Lucky Rabbit's Foot

A Fawn Malero Mystery

Courtney Davis

Copyright © 2023, Courtney Davis

Published by:
DX Varos Publishing
7665 E. Eastman Ave. #B101
Denver, CO 80231

This book contains material protected under International and Federal Copyright Laws and Treaties. Any unauthorized reprint or use of this material is prohibited. No part of this book may be reproduced or transmitted in any form or by any means, electronic or mechanical, including photocopying, recording, or by any information storage and retrieval system without express written permission from the author.

Book cover design and layout by Ellie Bockert Augsburger of Creative Digital Studios.
www.CreativeDigitalStudios.com

Cover design features:
Full size profile portrait of pretty lady running jump empty space toothy smile isolated on blue color background By deagreez; Cute white rabbits in various poses. Rabbit animal icon isolated on background. By Safyna; Snow caps, snowy ice and frozen icicles, vector cartoon icons, isolated on transparent background. Abstract snow frost caps and icicles of house roof shape for Christmas and New Year elements design By Sensvector; Dirt and debris on beach and in park, rubbish on ground and sand, vector flat cartoon illustration. Garbage in nature, polluted environment. Litter on seashore, river bank, at city parkland By Sensvector; Cat silhouette vector. Cat vector art, icon, and vector images. By vector - shop

ISBN: 978-1-955065-89-4 (paperback)
ISBN: 978-1-955065-90-0 (ebook)

Printed in the United States of America
ALL RIGHTS RESERVED

Thank you

To my family for the support they have given me in pursuit of this dream. You are my life but writing is my passion. I would never be able to pursue it without you all giving me the gift of time.

Chapter 1

I was *not* going to admit that I was in over my head. I was in charge of this part of Seattle and it being overrun by rabbits should have been well within my abilities. I was a magician who could communicate with animals! So why was every rabbit in town suddenly refusing to speak to me? I couldn't help but take it a little personally.

I didn't know if it was a trick being played by someone else, or if it was just dumb luck, but either way, they weren't talking and that meant the furry menaces were everywhere and I had no idea why. I also had no idea how to get rid of them, not that animal control was my job. I was a P.I. for supernaturals and in charge of keeping peace over a small portion of Seattle.

Currently a rabbit-infested portion of Seattle.

It just irked me that I couldn't easily solve this issue that should have been right up my alley. My brothers took great pleasure in reminding me of it too, the one time my abilities could have been so useful, and I had nothing to offer.

"What are you going to do with this batch?" Annabel asked as I shoved one more rabbit into a carrier cage with about twenty of its friends. I'd called in my half-Witch friend because I hoped her or her coven could tell me something about the situation that I was missing. Was there a magical element here that I just couldn't detect?

Unfortunately, Annabel couldn't get any sense of magic off of the things either, so she was just here helping round them up so I could take them somewhere outside of the city and drop them off. She wasn't exactly dressed to be helpful though, in skintight black jeans, a purple mesh top and a number of bracelets on each arm that even I had to raise an eyebrow at, and I like flashy. Her short black hair was styled to cover her pointy ears that indicated her elf father, and her purple eyes were rimmed in heavy black makeup. She looked like she was heading to a meeting of the occult. She frowned at a rabbit that ran out in front of her, making no effort at all to capture the thing for me.

"The pet store won't take any more," I grumbled, wiping my hands on my jeans. Catching rabbits was hard work and my once nice jeans and t-shirt were now covered in grass stains. "They didn't tell Betina why, just said no. I'm guessing no one wants to buy them because they can just walk down the street and take as many as they want." I huffed and pulled my light brown locks up into a quick bun so my neck could cool. It was unusually warm for October, which was a whole other problem Seattle had been dealing with.

The rabbit issue had started three weeks ago and every day I got phone calls from my brothers asking for an update I didn't have. And although my father had only checked in twice, I knew he was not happy with the possibility of having to get someone else involved to take care of this. Not that it was necessarily a supernatural problem, but it seemed too weird to be human made. No truck on its way to the bunny farm had tipped over on the freeway and spilled its furry cargo.

If supes were complaining about the infestation, they would be complaining to my father because he's in charge of the entire Seattle area and it's supernatural inhabitants. This would make it my problem by association to at least look into. I'd set myself up as a supernatural problem solver when I'd declared myself a P.I. capable of solving any mystery in the area.

"To the mountains then?" Annabel suggested. She poked a bunny that was hopping close with the toe of her black boot and tucked a lock of hair behind her pointy ear. "I'm not dressed for traipsing through the wilderness but if we just pull off the road and dump them maybe? You've tried *all* the pet stores?"

I sighed heavily as I hefted the cage into the backseat of my car. "I had Betina making calls all morning, no one wants any more." I didn't want Logan to come home and eat the problem but as I watched two more come around the house, I wasn't sure my efforts were doing any good.

Every day that passed I started thinking Logan's suggestion of calling in the pack to devour them all in one night was a good idea. Even though it turned my stomach.

Being able to communicate with animals had made me a vegetarian early in life. Though, if these rabbits wouldn't talk to me, did they really count as animals? I got as much feeling from them as I did a tomato plant.

I had to admit, this situation was getting out of hand. I didn't want to drive out of the city every day and dump loads of rabbits, barely making a dent in the problem. I had businesses to run, not only was I a P.I. for the supernatural, but I owned a yoga studio. I also hadn't visited Stephan for information on another supernatural object since the rabbits had shown up. Which meant I hadn't been able to charge my father for completing a job and bringing in a magical item the idiot had sold to a human in a while.

Stephan had been my introduction to the business unintentionally. He was a Magician who had gone against some of our most important laws, selling magical items to humans and letting our secret out. I'd caught him in Coeur d'Alene, Idaho and dragged him back here with Logan's help, and since then he's been allowed a stay of execution as long as he keeps telling me where to find some of the things he's sold. Because my father was in charge here, he had a prison in his basement and a responsibility to pay me for the service. It had been working out really great, until the rabbits started taking up all my free time.

"I just wish I knew what the hell was going on?" I said for the thousandth time.

Jasmine walked out of the house. She was a beautiful young magician that I'd been in love with as a teen. I watched her make her way across the yard in short shorts and a tank top, her blonde hair falling around her shoulders and her big green eyes shining. She smiled at me sweetly and I couldn't help feeling a pull to her that wasn't just about my supernatural empathy wanting to help out a Supe in trouble.

"The things give me the creeps, they are not normal," Jasmine said when she got to us. She gave a little shudder and rubbed her arms.

"Maybe your husband knows you don't like rabbits and sent them here to try and drive you back into his arms," Annabel suggested not so helpfully.

Jasmine just frowned and shook her foot at one that hopped too close. She'd run off from an emotionally controlling Warlock husband, pregnant and scared. She'd arrived on my doorstep and I think, had hoped to reignite our teenage fling, gaining my assistance. Unfortunately I wasn't interested in anything except helping her. A fact of which I'd had to reassure Logan multiple times. Typical controlling Werewolf, he didn't like any other potential or past lovers around me. But I had a supernatural empathetic drive that I couldn't ignore when it came to other Supes or animals. Another thing I didn't understand about these rabbits. I didn't feel the drive to help them, even when they were locked up in a carrier, I couldn't sense any distress.

"There's something off about them, even if there's no magic involved," I said. Watching another three hop out from under a bush and cross to the middle of the yard had me grinding my teeth. I really missed my dogs. They'd never let the things roam about the yard and my cats were no help at all.

My poor dogs had been murdered by one of my stalkers.

"I don't think Maddox is behind this, he wouldn't be so subtle," Jasmine said with a frown as she tugged nervously on a lock of her blonde hair.

I knew she was right about that. She'd received a threatening letter just the other day. He was going to come and retrieve her apparently whether she liked it or not. Over my dead body, I'd told her. He didn't deserve her, pregnant with his child or not and as long as she was under my roof, I was going to protect her with all I had. Which really wasn't a lot, but I had made some pretty powerful friends since embracing my supernatural side and that included a live-in bodyguard.

Betina was a teenager, but she was a Troll, not just a normal under-the-bridge, smelly, ugly one either. She was a warrior Troll, a breed that looked far more human actually but still tall and bulky. She still had the ability to stink on command and she was tough. Getting tougher too as she'd been training with Logan lately to improve her fighting skills. She'd be lean and lethal, rather than bulky and stiff like other Trolls tended to get.

Nothing was going to happen to Jasmine on our watch.

"Logan thinks we should be killing them." I just couldn't though, no matter how annoying, I couldn't kill these cute little things without proof that they were evil. "They haven't hurt anyone, they're just pests, eating everyone's fall gardens." Luckily it was mid-October, and most gardens were already done with their growing season, but my pumpkins had suffered.

Annabel gave me a look that said clearly, she agreed with Logan's plan. Jasmine gave a thoughtful hum as well.

"Not an option," I said firmly. I wasn't ready to give up on solving this one. "Who's coming with me to dump them outside of the city?"

"I'll join you; I don't have anything better to do," Annabel said with a shrug and another toe nudge to a rabbit that was getting close to her.

"I need a nap," Jasmine said with a dramatic yawn. I felt a tug at my empathy in response to her need. It had me think of making her soothing tea and tucking her in with a warm blanket on the couch.

I settled for a hug. "I don't like leaving you alone, maybe we should wait." Maddox could show up soon, unannounced, and cause her all kinds of stress that would be bad for the baby. Now that is a problem I wouldn't mind solving with teeth, maybe Logan could eat *him*.

"Don't worry, Betina should be home soon, she's the most kick ass teenager I've ever met," Jasmine said.

"Just lock the door, okay. I would wait, but I want to try and beat Logan home. He promised me a date night, vegetarian sushi and a stroll along the waterfront."

Jasmine gave me a knowing look. It was more than wanting to be in time for a date, I had tried to never let Logan and Jasmine be home without me to intervene. I was afraid they would fight and honestly, with Jasmine's abilities, either one of them could end up seriously hurt. Logan was very territorial, and it didn't matter that I'd assured them both I wasn't interested multiple times and Jasmine seemed to accept that fact, it still didn't soothe Logan's inner wolf apparently.

"Don't worry, I'll be nice," she said with a laugh. "I don't want to become wolf chow."

"Remember to lock the door and tell Evie to keep an eye out for strangers." Evie was my roommate, well my first roommate, now Betina lived with me pretty permanently, Jasmine was staying with me until she had another option, and Logan had basically moved in too. But Evie was a permanent fixture of the house. A ghost of an elderly woman who was very attached to the home because she'd lived there with her husband Albert for so many years. She'd never had any children and I think we all had become her unfinished business. She bossed us around, shamed us about our clothes, and my not being married to Logan. But she was always there so at least I could trust someone would be watching out while Jasmine took a nap and waited for Betina to get back from working at the yoga studio. Not that she could do anything to protect Jasmine, she'd at least be able to alert her to danger.

"Let's go," Annabel called as she slid into the passenger seat of my little car. "I have plans tonight that don't include bunnies."

"Oh, Annabel has a date!" I said with mock surprise and hurried to the car waving at Jasmine as she stood on the porch. "Who's the lucky guy or ghoul?" I prodded as I got in and started the car.

"Actually, I am having dinner with my father." She spoke without emotion, but I knew that she had a lot of feelings about her father, conflicting feelings. Witches were traditionally raised by their mothers, if she'd been a boy perhaps her mother would have sent her off to live with her father like they did when they bred with Warlocks, but Annabel's father was an Elf and that was different too.

You wouldn't know it to look at them, but Elves felt emotions deeply. They lived and looked calm and even. You would almost think they felt nothing, but it was their way of dealing with over feeling. Add that to the witches who were loud and crazy and basically off the wall sorority girls. Annabel had a mix of both and when she went inexpressive, I knew she was feeling lots of things.

She hadn't known her father at all until recently, even though his clan lived just north of Seattle on the peninsula near the ocean. Thanks to a little mystery having to do with the ocean, we'd paid him a visit at his Water Elf colony and although he'd known he had a daughter, that was the first time they'd met. He'd respected that the Witch's traditions or was simply afraid of Misty maybe. I wouldn't blame anyone for staying out of that Witch's way. I wanted to ask Annabel lots of questions but held back. I knew she would tell me if she wanted to and pressing would get me nowhere.

We drove in silence for a while, enjoying the oddly warm October sun, another thing that had me slightly worried. My mind drifted around the problems we were facing and coming up with no solutions.

"I think this is good," I said as I pulled off the main road.

"Looks as good as anything," Annabel agreed.

We got out of the car and looked around. No houses nearby, an expanse of wooded area for rabbits to enjoy.

They should be happy here. We pulled the cage out and opened it up, happy to see twenty rabbits hop off even though it was barely a dent in the problem. We would have to do this all day every day to even start to make a difference, and I couldn't do that, didn't want to do that. "We need a better solution," I grumbled and put the cage back in the car.

"No! You idiot," Annabel snapped as she chased a few rabbits away from the busy road.

"I thought you were pro killing them all," I said, barely containing my laughter as Annabel moved around like a goth pixie ushering helpless rabbits to safety.

"I'm pro killing the ones invading the city, these ones are now perfectly within their wild habitat and should stay alive and off the damn road."

I grunted in agreement and watched as they all seemed to wander a bit aimlessly. "You'd think they'd be running and hiding."

"Why, they don't run or hide in the city," Annabel pointed out.

"That's true, what the hell is wrong with them?" Something about their ambivalent behavior out in the wild made it seem odder. "There's definitely something weird about them."

"Yeah, they're probably a plague sent into the city to spy," she said with a laugh, but I didn't find it funny. I'd thought the exact thing more than once over the last few weeks. Annabel stood between one particularly determined rabbit and the road with her hands on her hips glaring at the thing. "Go," she hissed at it and finally it took a few hops away from her and started eating a piece of grass. Annabel looked at me then with a serious expression. "We can't keep this up."

"I know. There has to be a source and we have to find it. They are coming from somewhere, maybe we need to concentrate on that? Not worry about them individually, look at them as a whole? Though, why this is my problem, I still don't know. I'm not in animal control, I'm in magical item location and Sea Hag control, even harboring runaway pregnant Magicians is my job on occasion."

Annabel rolled her bright purple eyes at me. "You know why. You snap at your brothers every time they call to check in on the problem and that's because you *want* to solve this, and they know it too. You're good at figuring stuff out and this really should be easy for you. So own it, this is your problem. So where the hell do we go from here?"

I had no answer and that's why I'd been catching rabbits for the last week despite it being a useless task.

"We start back to the city," I said and got in the car.

Annabel got in the passenger seat and wiped grass off of her boots, throwing it out the window as I started to drive.

"Do you want to talk about what else is bothering you?" Annabel asked. It was her half Elf side that made her quite intuitive to the feelings of others, her Witch half made her nosey as hell about it.

"No." I would rather throw myself into the problem of the rabbits and ignore the tension at home. Logan was understandably uncomfortable with the situation despite my assurance that I wasn't interested in picking up with Jasmine where we'd left off. I also couldn't convince him that I held no lingering feelings for her, because I did. She was my first love and she's a wonderful, beautiful person. Not to mention her obvious need for help was hitting all my supernatural empathy buttons. But that didn't change the way I felt about Logan, and it didn't mean I wanted to be with her now, and he was just going to have to accept that because it *was* the truth.

Annabel didn't press, which I appreciated. She was nosey, and she was really a good listener, but she was respectful too. She knew that I would come to her if I needed to talk things out, until then she'd just watch and analyze from the sidelines.

"Do you want to talk about dinner with your father?" I asked to further distract her.

"No," she said and stared out the passenger window.

So we drove on in silence. It wasn't uncomfortable, we were both lost in our own thoughts and problems.

Chapter Two

"The fuck?" I breathed as a sudden wall of snow stood between us and the city. Traffic was sliding to a stop in front of us. This was way beyond what the drivers of Seattle could handle, especially randomly in October when it had been about seventy degrees when we'd left the house with the rabbits.

I gripped the wheel with both hands and we skidded to a stop just inches from the car in front of us. The car in the lane next to us wasn't as fortunate. There was an awful screech and scrape, then a crunch as it slid into a stopped van in front of it. Luckily it had been a slow motion crash and likely no one was injured. The cars would need work though and I was tempted to hand over a business card for Betina's boyfriend, Tony. He had done a great job buffing out and repainting my car recently. I was no longer driving around with the word *bitch* scratched into my driver's side door thanks to one of my recent stalkers.

"Again?" Annabel shouted, throwing her hands up in exasperation. "It was t-shirt weather when we left with the damn rabbits. Now I'll have to change, these boots were *not* made for snow."

This was just the latest in odd weather patterns we'd been experiencing lately. No one had any idea what was going on with it. My father said that even Stephan hadn't been able to admit to any magical item being sold that could do the things we'd seen lately. Yesterday it was a hundred-degree heat wave, last week, a small hurricane, though still strong enough to damage some boats and the Ferris wheel was out of commission for the time being, but luckily no serious damage or deaths had occurred. Rain had been too strong lately, wind extra harsh, and we'd been pounded by hot sun in between freak storms. It was starting to really worry the humans and the pressure was on to figure out what the fuck was happening. No one in the Supe community believed it wasn't magic in nature which made it very much my father's problem, being his city, which made it my problem because I was constantly trying to prove myself to him and my brothers. My brothers and I all had our own little piece of the city to take care of. Something affecting the whole thing, like this weather and the rabbits, was a problem for all of us. I would love to solve it first, it would really piss off my oldest brother, Rex. Of course, I had no more ideas about where to start with this thing than I did with the rabbits. It was without reason or pattern.

"Maybe this will force the rabbits into hibernation?" I said hopefully as traffic started to move again, very slowly. Not the lane next to us, they were out of their cars and arguing. At this rate it was going to be another hour before we got home, and Logan was definitely going to be there before me. Hopefully he would be nice.

"Do rabbits hibernate?" Annabel asked.

"They don't come into the city in droves, that's about all I know about the things."

Annabel laughed and I tried to borrow some of her joy for life in this moment when everything felt so fucked and out of control.

"This weather thing is worse than the rabbits, it's so inconsistent I don't even know where to start looking, or for what."

"Stephan didn't have any clues?"

"No, he told my father that he never sold any weather manipulation objects. Maybe he's off the hook for this one."

"Could it be a person and not an object?"

That was something I hadn't really considered. "Like just a Magician who controls the weather? Yeah, it's definitely possible but why here and now? And what the fuck is his problem? This is just being an asshole." There didn't seem to be any motivation or plan to the madness of the weather patterns. Unless someone was simply trying to make a mess out of the city, they were definitely succeeding in that, but what could be the point? "This kind of thing would get a magician locked up for a century, I don't see why anyone would risk that."

Annabel nodded. "My father said the Elf clan isn't experiencing anything like this, it seems to be contained in the city and just offshore. Could be someone who's trying to get attention maybe. Someone who doesn't understand the kind of trouble they'll be in when caught."

"He's got my attention, and the entire fucking city's attention. So why is he hiding? When is he going to come out with his demands or to say *Ha, got ya*!"

"Why do you think it's a he?"

I frowned, I couldn't really say, but it was an asshole thing to do so I just assumed a guy was behind it. "Alright, he or she is an ass and needs to come out with what they want already so I can take them down. If its attention, they have it, if it's some kind of power play... well that would be bad. Some Magician looking to take over Seattle from my father?" I bit my lip as that idea took root. Could this be a coup? My father was very powerful and well liked, but that didn't make him untouchable. "It would make more sense if they'd try to get in on Portland, that city didn't even have a Magician in control."

"Let's not get out of hand, think logically. There's not enough of a pattern to find an origination point, which probably means whoever it is moves around when they instigate. So it's probably not a Witch or Warlock, that would take a whole spell with lots of prep. You can't just do that anywhere," Annabel reasoned.

"You seem pretty quick to think it's a Supe, what if a human is behind it, just like the ocean thing. Shit," a thought popped into my head. "What if it is coming from the ocean? Don't a lot of weather patterns develop because of the ocean?"

Annabel looked thoughtful. "Yeah, I think so, to a point, but why would an ocean Supe be interested in the weather in the city?"

I didn't have an answer for that, but it was worth checking out. "Maybe you can contact your boytoy Siren and find out if they've noticed anything weird under the water."

Annabel's cheeks reddened slightly. "I haven't talked to Jason since I left his cave."

"Because..." I pressed, knowing my friend had spent a few wild nights with the sexy Siren then refused to give up any juicy details about it. I was dying to know what sex with a Siren was like, what sex underwater was like! She'd been uncharacteristically closed lipped about the whole thing.

She rolled her eyes. "Because he was getting clingy."

I laughed; I couldn't help myself. "You're just afraid you might actually like him," I teased.

"We can contact *someone* from the ocean if my father doesn't think it's a ridiculous ask, but I'm not seeking out Jason."

"Deal."

She looked out the passenger window. "He sang during sex," she said almost too quiet for me to hear.

I jerked the wheel a little as I darted my eyes to her. "What?"

She groaned and put her hands over her face. "He sang during sex; you know like his whole Siren song shit they do. It was weird!"

"Like love songs? He was serenading you?" I asked and tried very hard to keep the amusement out of my tone. I'd fallen for his song, almost drowned because of it. But what I remember was just a noise, no words but it was so beautiful I'd wanted to wrap myself in it. Sirens were beautiful but no stronger than a human who worked out. Their songs incapacitated their victims and made them easy to kill or get away from depending on what the goal was. They weren't evil, but they deserved a way to protect themselves, everyone did.

"It was a language I didn't fucking understand, he could have been saying anything. Maybe he was reciting the alphabet to keep from early ejaculation. I don't fucking know, but I'm telling you, it was weird, and distracting, and I don't think I could make a life with a guy who had to sing to get off, or not get off..."

"Make a life with. That's not a very Witch thing to say." Witches loved em and left em. They were willing to take the sperm, raise a female child, a male maybe for a year or two, but that was about it. They lived in large coven houses with each other. Loud music, loud voices, and no men.

Annabel stared out the passenger window and was silent for a couple slow icy miles. "I don't think I want what Tara has."

"A half Werewolf baby?" I was a little offended, knowing that's what I was looking at with Logan. Tara was a Witch in Annabel's coven, and she'd been briefly married to an abusive Wolf in Logan's pack. She was now raising the baby with her coven and the father was dead, not just for being abusive to her, but also for trying to kidnap me, a couple times actually.

"No, not the wolf thing, the alone thing. It would have been nice to know my Elf half growing up. I don't necessarily want a live in, I know that's probably not my nature, but I want something close I think."

I was shocked, but it was understandable. "Well, maybe Jason isn't your soulmate. That's okay, what about your father's clan? Any eligible bachelors there? It might make sense to have a kid with an Elf since you're half. I bet it would be adorable."

"I haven't met any young men in his clan, he has only introduced me to old married people. I think he's afraid I'll corrupt the youth of his clan." She laughed like the thought was right on and she didn't care one bit. That was her Witch half for sure.

"I could see that," I laughed. "Well, no Jason but maybe we can take a boat ride tonight and at least see if the ocean Supes have any ideas for us."

"Probably worth checking, but I'll ask my father first, he might know something we don't, and he wouldn't tell me without prompting." Elves didn't just offer up information.

"There doesn't seem to be a specific target, just chaos," I muttered as the slick roads caused more accidents all around us and I managed to avoid more than one car doing to the slow slide in my direction. I had no interest in getting into an accident, I could heal faster than a human, but I could break just as easily.

Annabel's phone rang as we got close to the city, about an hour later than we should have been. I listened in as she apologized to her father for being late and he arranged to meet her at my house instead.

"I hope you don't mind," Annabel said as she hung up.

As if I had a choice apparently. "Not at all. Fanlin will be a great buffer between Logan and Jasmine." Maybe the weather caught Logan out too, maybe he had to be a good citizen and push old ladies out of the ditch or something and hasn't spent an hour glaring at Jasmine in my living room.

Annabel gave me a sardonic look. "Sure, until he comments about the feelings of love and desire wafting off of Jasmine in response to you."

I glared out the front window. The first time I met Fanlin was with Logan by my side, and we hadn't exactly figured out how we felt about each other yet. Fanlin had casually called me Logan's mate based on the feelings he sensed in him.

Shit. I stepped on the gas and my tail end swerved. We barely missed the ditch and a little red truck as I straightened the car back out. The snow was finally melting, and I needed to get home, maybe send Logan on an errand that would take a few hours.

Annabel gripped the door handle and glared at me. "Fuck, Fawn you need to chill. Logan won't eat your girlfriend."

I wish I could be that sure. "She's just a friend."

Annabel rolled her eyes. "There's nothing wrong with having feelings for someone else when you're in a relationship, Fawn. The wrong comes when you act on it without permission from your partner. Shit, maybe Logan would be into it," she said with a lascivious grin.

I knew she was trying to get a rise out of me, so I didn't respond. I had no interest in rekindling a relationship with Jasmine, which Annabel knew, we'd talked about it thoroughly. But I did care deeply for her, as an old friend, as a first love, and as a Supe in trouble.

When it became obvious I wasn't going to rise to her bait Annabel sat back and relaxed a bit. Not completely, but that could have more to do with her father waiting for her than my excellent slushy road driving.

By the time we were pulling into my garage the snow was merely a wet mess and a few rabbits were again hopping about. I smiled as the door shut, blocking out a couple curious creatures that were sniffing in the driveway. One stopped and lifted its head, it was mostly white with one black spot right over its left eye and one of its floppy ears was grey. The damn thing stared straight into my rearview mirror as if it was seeing me before the door blocked his view. That was different.

The door into the house opened then and Evie stood there with a huge smile, dressed in a pair of beige slacks and a surprisingly flashy red top. Her grey hair was in a loose twist with a few tendrils around her face.

"I'm guessing that means Fanlin is here," I said with a laugh. Evie loved when handsome men were in the house and she always dressed for the occasion. She may be a ghost, but her libido seemed to be alive and well. Which made her shaming of me all the more frustrating.

"Have you thought about my grandmother's offer to get rid of her?" Annabel joked as she got out of the car, loud enough for Evie to hear and scowl in response. Evie didn't admit what she was, but I had gotten a feeling recently that she knew a lot more than she let on. She also pretended she had no idea what we all were and she hated it when anyone treated her like she wasn't a living breathing member of the household.

"I'm not sure I would know what to do without her creeping around the house," I said honestly.

"I'm glad you're back, it's rude to keep men waiting," Evie said, Pointedly ignoring both our comments.

"Men? Is Logan here already?" I hadn't seen his truck out front and assumed he'd been stuck in traffic the same as me. Hoped really.

"No," Evie said with bright eyes, and I became instantly wary. She popped away before I had a chance to ask her to explain.

I looked at Annabel, she just shrugged.

It wasn't unusual for Supes to show up on my doorstep for help. I hurried inside expecting to find someone in need. We were greeted by Fanlin and an Elf I'd never met before standing in my living room. The new Elf was handsome, in a stoic sort of way. Tall and lean, with the traditional white hair of an Elf and silvery blue eyes that all the Water Elves seemed to have. He was currently dressed to blend with humans in jeans and a button up white linen shirt rather than the flowing pants and tunic Fanlin wore. I don't think I'd ever seen Fanlin in anything else. I might faint if I saw him in something as human as jeans.

Elves were the least likely out of all the Supes to be found mixed with humans. They kept to themselves in hidden communities and relied on Magicians like my father to be their go between when needed. Not only did they not look human with their eyes and pointy ears, but they refused to act like humans when needed.

"Daughter, I'd like you to meet Gildar." Fanlin presented the man like a prize she had won, he even swept a hand like a car show model as he said the guy's name.

Annabel didn't miss the meaning behind this introduction, and she narrowed her eyes at her father, ignoring Gildar's outstretched hand.

Jasmine, who was lounging on the couch with Pumpkin, my big orange cat in her lap, choked back a laugh. I shot her a look to tell her to shut it and she winked at me.

"Blind dates are not my thing," Annabel said calmly. Her stiff shoulders and fisted hands contradicting that calm she was trying to project.

"Oh no, you misunderstand," Gildar said quickly and stepped forward. "I am not blind; I see very well and think you are quite beautiful despite your dark hair."

I couldn't hold back my giggle and Jasmine snorted behind me. I'm pretty sure I saw Fanlin roll his eyes, if the tiny movement could be considered such a huge show of emotion from the Elf. Annabel looked like she was about to throw some kind of jock itch spell at the poor guy and Evie watched with open mouthed shock.

Fanlin put a hand on Gildar's shoulder, stopping him from saying anything else. "Gildar is the son of a good friend of mine. They have a clan north of mine and he has come to visit in search of new blood for his clan. I thought you two would enjoy meeting each other," Fanlin explained.

"Why?" Annabel demanded.

"Because you are of similar age and both single."

"So you *are* trying to set us up. New blood? Is that what I am? Is that why you bred with my mother?" Annabel hissed. "Because she wasn't already part of your inbred clan?"

I stepped closer to Annabel. Despite my desire to get farther away from the emotional Witch, I would offer her my moral support because she was my friend, and I didn't want her to do something she'd regret. This was a very poorly planned meeting on Fanlin's part, and it was probably a good thing it was happening in my living room rather than the restaurant with human witnesses.

Poor Gildar looked confused. I had a feeling there wasn't a lot going on inside that pretty head of his. He looked from Fanlin to Annabel with a slight frown.

"I wanted you to meet, yes," Fanlin said, ignoring her other accusations.

"I'm busy. Fawn and I were going out to meet Jason."

Were we? I just gave a stiff nod.

"The Siren boy?" Fanlin asked stiffly.

His reaction made it obvious that he knew Annabel had spent a few nights with Jason, perhaps rumors traveled quickly among the water Supes. Apparently, he didn't approve.

"I wanted to find out if the ocean Supes had any ideas about what might be causing these weird weather patterns," I explained.

His gaze shot to me.

"We were going to ask you as well," I added quickly, hoping I wasn't offending him.

"I don't know of anything, but it wouldn't hurt to ask someone below the water I suppose. Gildar will accompany you, he has experience dealing with the ocean Supes."

"So do we," Annabel gritted out, but Fanlin acted as if he didn't hear her.

"And besides, it will be good to have a male with you for protection."

My eyes traveled over Gildar's thin physique doubtfully. Of course I was used to a Werewolf protecting me from big bads. Logan was wide and bulky compared to this guy. "I appreciate the thought, but we weren't going out alone. Betina and Tony will be with us," I explained, hoping to diffuse the situation a bit.

"Nonsense, he needs to make himself useful," Fanlin said with a surprising amount of gruff, then started to walk toward the door.

I was about to panic. He was *not* leaving this guy here! But the door opened before he got there and in walked Logan with a fierce look on his face and a bleeding arm; completely distracting me from anything else.

"What the hell happened?" I gasped and ran for him, all my instincts to help and heal kicked in along with my girlfriend instincts to love and soothe.

"Got in an argument with a rabbit on your front porch."

I grabbed his good arm and pulled him into the kitchen. "Is it a bite?" I asked as I ran his arm under the faucet. I needed to determine how bad it was. Did he need stitches or just a bandage? My fingers tingled as they touched his injured arm.

"I hope you don't have rabies now. Rabid Werewolves seems like a big problem, we'll have to put you down," Jasmine called from the living room.

Logan growled and met my eyes with a frown. I waited for him to answer the question, it was a valid ask. So far none of the rabbits had given any indication of being violent, of course they might react differently to a predator like Logan versus me. Animals naturally trusted me.

"Scratches," Logan said. "He didn't like the way I was removing him from your property I guess."

"Maybe he wanted to come inside," Evie suggested. "It is cold and wet out there."

"Warming quickly," Logan said. "The damn things have fur, they're fine. Or maybe they should leave if they don't like it."

I dabbed at the wound, which was surprisingly deep, but I knew he'd heal fast, Werewolves were great at that.

"Just a scratch, no rabies but we should clean it properly, so you don't have to deal with an infection."

Logan grabbed my chin with his free hand and forced me to look into his deep brown eyes. I relaxed and filled with a comfortable heat. "I'm fine," he whispered and kissed me quickly. "But I'll let you clean any part of me you want to," he whispered against my lips. "When we're alone."

I giggled and pulled away, my cheeks heating a bit. I dried off the wound and that was all he would allow. He grabbed a paper towel and held it over the oozing scratches.

Chester chirped a hello as he flew in then and landed on the counter. The parakeet hadn't been the same since his best friend was killed, Jake my chocolate lab.

"Bird's hungry," Evie said.

"Too bad you weren't home all day and able to feed him, huh," I grumbled and looked up at Logan. "I think it needs to be covered, at least for tonight." If nothing else, it would remind him to be careful and not reopen the healing wound.

"Whatever the nurse orders," Logan said with a sly grin.

"Horny Werewolf," I teased and gave him a quick kiss before I went for the first aid kit in the downstairs bathroom.

As I spread a little cream over the scratches and slapped on a cover, I realized Fanlin was gone and Betina and her boyfriend, Tony, were now in the living room with Gildar.

"When did Fanlin leave?" I asked.

"Snuck out while you were fussing with my arm under the faucet. Who's the Elf he left behind?"

"A suitor," I whispered. "Gildar."

"For Annabel I hope," Logan growled low.

"Yeah, I already have plenty," I said with a wink and patted his now bandaged arm. I cleaned up the mess and Annabel walked into the kitchen looking like she was ready to explode.

"So what's with the extra Elf?" Logan asked, as if he didn't already know.

"My father is trying to set us up," she hissed.

"So he just leaves him here? Bold move," Logan said as if he thought it was a good one.

"Apparently my father has decided I need protection, Gildar is my *bodyguard* until the weather and rabbit issues are solved." She shot me a look to indicate this whole Gildar thing was now my problem too. Great.

"Fanlin must think something major is happening if he left you a bodyguard," I pointed out. "That's not comforting, do you think he's not telling us something?"

"Or he's just using it as an excuse to push me and Gildar together. As if this is some kind of fucking romance novel. I tell you what though, there's no way I can take him to the coven house, my mother will freak."

I gritted my teeth and looked at the Elf knowing I couldn't kick him out. "He can stay here," I sighed. "He can take the basement, Betina prefers the couch anyway."

Logan's chest rumbled but he didn't say anything. He was used to me taking in strays at this point, he just preferred it when they were female. Aside from Jasmine anyway.

"Thank you, Fawn," Annabel said. "And hey, maybe he'll fall in love with Jasmine."

Logan grunted.

"Jasmine doesn't need a man, she needs a divorce," I pointed out. "But if he's willing to play bodyguard for her too, that would be nice. I don't like leaving her alone."

We all turned to look at Gildar who was pushing Sofia, my Siamese cat away with a toe. He was perched on the edge of a chair looking stiff and uncomfortable. Nothing about him indicated bodyguard. If it wasn't for the height advantage, I think I could take him down.

"Well, maybe he can at least be another set of eyes out for her ex showing up," I amended.

"We *have* established that he isn't blind," Annabel said brightly, and we both laughed, hard.

"I missed something," Logan said, and we nodded as we tried to gather ourselves back up while everyone in the living room looked at us with curious eyes.

"Okay," I said, taking a deep breath and wiping a happy tear from my eye. "We want to go out and ask the ocean Supes if they have any idea what we might be looking for with this weather thing."

"Boat trip, huh," Logan said.

"We have nothing else to go on so it's worth checking out," I said.

"Does Tony know?" Logan asked.

"Does Tony know what?" Tony called from the living room.

"Can we borrow a boat?" I asked and gave him a bright smile. Tony owned a shop near the water where he fixed boats mostly, but cars too. He'd taken us out more than once on a borrowed boat and as much as I hated to ask again, I knew we needed to do it.

"As if I would turn down the powerful Fawn Malero," he said dramatically.

Chapter Three

An hour later; me, Logan, Annabel, Gildar, and Tony were headed out into the sound in a borrowed boat. This scenario was more common than I ever would have expected, and I needed to do something nice for Tony so he didn't think I wasn't appreciative. Betina had stayed home to keep Jasmine safe, which she wasn't happy about, but Gildar refused to even consider letting Annabel go out on her own so it had been the next best option.

It wasn't snowing but it was still a cold October night. Luckily Tony was a Warlock with a wonderful ability to spread a warmth out around him, so we all didn't freeze as we sped along. I, of course, was cuddled up close to Logan anyway. Werewolves ran hot and I wasn't above using him for his body heat. Annabel was, of course, sitting as far from Gildar as possible.

It was nice compared to the drive over. It had been tight and awkward in Logan's truck. Gildar had nearly thrown Tony out of the way to slide in the back next to Annabel. I wasn't sure if he was just taking his duty as bodyguard seriously or if he was worried Tony was going to move in on his girl, but it didn't make Annabel happy and the rest of us weren't sure what to say.

"Are you slipping in again this time? The water's damn cold," Tony asked Annabel as the boat idled to a stop.

"I don't know any other way to call someone up to answer questions," Annabel said with a sigh and started to strip. She hadn't been prepared and so there was no bathing suit under her clothes, but she stripped down to her bra and panties without shame. Not that she had anything to be embarrassed about, she had a beautiful fit body and her black bralette and panties covered enough to be decent. Gildar stared the whole time like a fool while Tony and Logan were carefully looking the other way.

Annabel jumped into the water and Gildar gasped.

"I bet Jason answers first," I said.

Gildar spun to look at me. "Is this her boyfriend?"

"They have history," I explained.

"I am to make her my wife," he said and frowned down into the dark water.

I looked at Logan hoping he could butt in and explain that Gildar might need to chill, no matter what Fanlin had told him. Logan just shrugged, Gildar wasn't our problem, not really.

We waited in uncomfortable silence after that. Logan kept me tight against him and I enjoyed the moment as best I could. I almost felt bad for Gildar though, he looked like a lost puppy waiting for Annabel to pop back up.

"You're not a full Elf," I said without thinking. He was showing far too much emotion to be.

His cheeks reddened and he shook his head. "No, my mother is a Witch."

That explained a lot. Fanlin probably thought the two half Elf, half Witches were a match made in heaven.

"I was raised in the Elf colony with my father," Gildar said.

Which probably meant he'd been very sheltered from human life and would have a hard time blending. A hard time understanding that Annabel was under no obligation to marry anyone just because her father thought it was a good idea.

Great.

After a few minutes, Annabel surfaced and gasped for air. She was able to hold her breath under water for quite a while, thanks to her parentage, but not indefinitely. She climbed aboard with Gildar's assistance.

"Got someone," she said and wrapped a towel around herself.

"You shouldn't take such risks," Gildar chastised.

"You should shut up," Annabel snapped, "Jason's on his way, I'm pretty sure."

I didn't ask how she knew it was Jason and not someone else, but I wasn't surprised, she did know the man intimately. Though I was a little disappointed, it would be nice to see Eldoris or Bay again.

"Jason has history with you," Gildar said flatly.

"Yeah, not that it is any of your business," Annabel hissed and glared at me.

"He asked," I said with a shrug. "And I think even he could have figured that one out on his own."

Tony covered a laugh with a cough and I felt a little bad for making fun of the Elf. It wasn't his fault he seemed a little naive.

Water rippled and up popped a blond head followed by two bright blue eyes. He floated all the way up until his entire muscled and tan torso was out of the water, then he rushed forward to the boat and grasped the side. "Annabel! I have missed you!"

"Yeah," she drawled. "I've been busy," Annabel said.

Gildar moved close behind her and looked disdainfully at Jason. "We have questions for you, Siren."

"Who the fuck are you?" Jason demanded and rose higher, his eyes flashing angrily.

I looked at Logan, he needed to assert his Alpha assholiness and stop any fights from breaking out on a boat in the middle of the sound.

Logan rolled his eyes but stepped forward with a confident swagger and cleared his throat. "Jason, we are here in an official capacity. Fawn Malero needs to know if you've noticed anything odd under the water like the weather we are having up here. Is it affecting anything below the surface and is there anything in the ocean Supe's lore about things that can control the weather?"

"We've noticed the problem," he said. "It has fluctuated our water temperatures more than usual and caused some unusual migrations in some of the fish. We don't know of anything that controls weather patterns like that though, I'm sorry I don't have more information." He made a quick move and lifted his very naked body up onto the boat.

Sirens were human in form and proud of it, standing with his chest puffed out and hands on his hips, dick swinging. I averted my eyes, of course... but it was there, and it was obvious. I really wished Annabel would share a few more details about her time with this golden god of a man.

"I will assist in solving the problem because my love has asked me to," Jason said.

There was a moment of shocked silence at his statement. Followed by a sound of anger from Gildar and outraged hissing from Annabel. I looked at Logan, pleading for him to intervene, but he just watched with an amused tilt to his lips.

"Don't damage the borrowed boat," Tony said quietly but made no move to step into the middle of the glaring threesome.

"No one here is your anything and we don't need or want your help, but thanks," Annabel snapped.

Jason reached out and pulled her to him, but before he could kiss her as he obviously intended, Gildar punched him. The move was unexpected, and Jason did nothing to block the surprisingly powerful blow. The poor guy crumpled unconscious on the bottom of the boat.

"What the hell, Gildar?" Annabel hissed.

Tony and Logan had quickly moved to restrain the Elf if necessary, placing themselves between Gildar and Jason. But Gildar just stood there with his hands at his sides and a calm expression on his face.

"He was going to kiss you against your wishes," Gildar said.

Annabel's eyes flashed with something I thought might have been appreciation, but she quickly tamped it down. "I'm a big girl, I can take care of myself." Annabel knelt beside Jason and brushed back his hair. "Why isn't he waking up?"

"Oh, I spelled him to stay knocked out for a few hours," Gildar admitted sheepishly.

"That's one way to win a fight," Logan said and moved away. Tony grunted in agreement.

"A spell?" Annabel asked, looking up at Gildar as she put her hands on Jason's head. I knelt next to the downed Siren as well, putting my hands on him to try and get a feel for his injuries.

"My mother is a Witch, I know a few things."

Annabel turned back to Jason. "That explains a lot," she said. "My father doesn't think I'm a good match for a full Elf, huh."

Her last words were so quiet I think I was the only one who heard them. "Oh Annabel," I said, meeting her gaze over the passed-out Siren. She just shook her head and stood up.

"Let's get out of here, can we dump him back in the water?" Annabel asked.

"I don't know, with the spell and everything. I wouldn't want him to drown because of us," I pointed out.

"Great, well he wanted to help so bring him along I guess," Annabel said.

I looked at Logan who was currently watching Gildar with a wary eye.

"Fine," I said. "He isn't dying, just asleep as far as I can tell. Let's take him back and hope he's up before we dock."

"He won't be," Gildar said happily, and I didn't hold back my best death glare.

He frowned at me and went to sit down, looking a bit like a petulant child.

Logan threw a towel over Jason's lower half as the boat started to drive off.

The boat ride back to the dock was silent and I vacillated between thinking we should arrest Gildar for the attack and thinking this jealous interaction was just hilarious. Annabel didn't look amused however, and when we got to the dock, she insisted Gildar could *not* stay with me because obviously Jason was going to have to be nursed back to health by me. He wasn't injured, I was pretty sure, though I didn't point that out. The spell would wear off and he might have a sore cheek, that's it.

"Great, I will stay with you, I will keep you safe," Gildar said with a bright smile.

"Oh no, that was *not* an invitation. I don't want or need you anywhere near me," Annabel hissed.

"And where do you expect him to stay?" I asked.

"Fuck if I care, he can go back to the Elf clan and tell my father I rejected his half-Elf suitor."

I glanced at Gildar and saw his face fall. "I can't go back a failure."

"I'm not interested," Annabel insisted. "You didn't fail, you just... aren't my type. Hell, I don't even know you."

"Yes," Gildar said brightly. "You don't know me, but you will. I will protect you and you will get to know me, and you will love me."

Annabel's face filled with anger and her eyes narrowed. She looked like she was about to throw a lethal spell at the poor guy.

Luckily Tony noticed too. "He can stay with me, my sister is visiting her father's clan for a few days anyway," Tony offered.

I sighed in relief. "Thank you!" I gave Tony a warm smile, he really was a great guy, and I was so glad he and Betina had hit it off despite her being a few years younger and literally just out of the cave.

"But I am to protect you, Annabel," Gildar insisted.

"Yeah, I don't need protection. You can hang with Tony until Fanlin comes to collect you."

"I will not. I will sleep outside your coven house if I must. I have a duty," Gildar insisted.

Annabel looked like she was about to explode. Tony put an arm around Gildar. "Come on, I'll show you where you can sleep tonight. You're welcome to stalk Annabel tomorrow."

"Fine," Gildar said dejectedly.

Relieved for the time being, I turned to our other problem. Logan currently had Jason cradled in his arms like a damsel in distress. At least he'd kept the towel wrapped around the Siren's waist.

"Take me home," I said, giving Logan's arm a pat and grabbing Annabel's arm as we walked to Logan's truck. Logan put the Siren in the back seat, Annabel and I sat up front with Logan.

"What was my father thinking?" Annabel said as we drove off.

"He's half Witch, your father probably thought it was an obvious great match." I cringed a little as I said it, knowing how she was taking it.

"So why tell him that he needs to protect me?"

That I couldn't explain. It felt like such an obvious set up, the protection order had to just be an excuse, though Gildar seemed like he sincerely believed it was necessary too.

"Do you think he knows something we don't?" I asked.

"About this weather crap, or the rabbits?" Annabel asked.

I glanced at Logan's bandaged arm. "Either, both maybe."

"He's not the type to hold back information for no reason. If he knew, he'd tell us," Annabel said.

"So he might just be a concerned father," I pointed out.

"Or it's just a misplaced setup attempt," Annabel gritted out.

"Because you're more into that?" Logan asked, pointing into the back seat.

"No," Annabel said, her cheeks reddening.

"Hard to please," Logan grunted.

"And there's nothing wrong with that," I offered. Annabel didn't need a man in her life to be happy, no one did.

When we arrived back at my place, I wasn't surprised to find Zin's sleek car parked out front. She and Drake were regular nighttime visitors. Coming over after the sun went down, unless Zin was working at my yoga studio that evening. I'd turned it into a surprisingly lucrative twenty-four-hour business, catering to vampires and other Supes at night. Zin was Logan's adopted sister and had become one of my best friends and nighttime manager. Drake was much older and her boyfriend, who everyone assumed would end up with a broken heart because of Zin. She was young and full of life, ready to discover love and what life had to offer. Drake had lost a wife and child years and years ago and had spent his recent life moping and carrying out orders made by his powerful father, Cassius Vamprose.

"Take him to the basement I guess, hopefully he doesn't freak out whenever this wears off. Wait, do you think he needs to sleep in water, like Eldoris?" Eldoris, an octopus shifter had stayed with me for a time and preferred sleeping in my bathtub full of saltwater.

"I think he'll be fine; he doesn't live in water a hundred percent of the time and has a regular type of bedroom in a cave," Annabel said and I quirked an eyebrow at her. She just rolled her eyes.

Logan carried Jason into the house and down to the basement, gasps of delight from Evie, Jasmine, and Betina followed him.

"Always bringing in strays," Zin teased as she embraced me. Her pixie cut black hair was smoothed to her head tonight and held back partially with a silver clip with little fangs on it.

"This one's Annabel's fault," I said.

"Why is he naked?" Evie asked with concern. "And who hurt the poor dear?"

"Gildar punched him for trying to kiss Annabel. He's naked because ocean Supes don't wear clothes," I explained.

In typical Evie style, she ignored the part that didn't fit her script for the world and focused on the punching. "Annabel, you know it's bad form to have men fight physically for your affection."

Annabel glared at the ghost. "Oh yeah, what kind of fighting should they do?"

Evie got a wistful look on her face. "They should fight with words, poetry, and presents to win you over, of course."

"I suppose they should do it on horseback too, old woman," Annabel grunted.

"Don't be ridiculous," Evie said and disappeared. I was willing to bet she was down in the basement peeking at the naked guest.

Jasmine hurried past with an armload of blankets and what I think were some of Logan's clothes. It made sense to take something down for him to wear, so I didn't complain. Drake followed, out of curiosity or to help I wasn't sure.

"What are you two up to tonight?" I asked Zin, eyeing her outfit. She was dressed to kill in a black minidress with thigh high boots and lots of skin showing.

"Cassius is getting into town tonight. We are checking out the wedding facilities with him." Zin didn't sound thrilled.

Cassius Vamprose was the leader of the North American Vampires and a very scary, very important Vampire. I had no interest in meeting him. His middle son, Drake, was an amazing man, the second Vampire I ever trusted, Zin being the first. Of course it had helped that she'd been raised by Werewolves and didn't act like a typical Vampire. Or maybe she did, and I just had let some of my prejudice go by the time I met her.

"Oh, the wedding party is coming in tonight?" I asked, trying to sound casual. That would mean Logan's ex-fiancé, Anthea, and her father, Drake's brother, would be in town too..

Dante, he was a Vampire that invaded far too many of my deep dark thoughts and feelings. I shivered at the thought of him being so close to me again. Would he reach out into my mind while I slept? I swear he pushed his dirty passionate dreams on me, though I could neither prove it, nor accuse him without embarrassing myself.

Anthea had decided to have her wedding here in Seattle over Halloween, I have no idea why she chose my city. We were going to attend because Logan was expected as representative of the local Werewolf pack. He had newly inherited the alpha position after his father's death at his brother, Cole's, hands. He was another of my recent stalkers. I wasn't going to let Logan attend his ex-fiancé's wedding alone so I would have to face Dante and his scary father whether I wanted to or not.

"They'll all be here tomorrow actually. Cassius came early and is already grumbling about the problems the city is having. He doesn't understand why his granddaughter would want to have her wedding here, it's not nearly as sophisticated and showy as he wants for the European Vamps, so he's trying to make it as acceptable as possible. He's invited a lot of important people and he's worried this will reflect poorly on him." Zin leaned in to whisper, although in a room full of Supes no whisper was ever completely hidden. "Maybe they'll decide to hold the wedding somewhere else," Zin said.

"Wouldn't that be a shame," I said sarcastically. Having Anthea or Dante in my town again was not something I looked forward to. I wasn't normally a jealous person, but Anthea was adorable. She had porcelain white skin, deep red lips, bright blue eyes, and she turned into a bat! That had to appeal to a man who also turned into an animal. The first time I'd met her she'd still thought she was engaged to Logan despite me being in a relationship with him and her being engaged to someone else. I know they'd been young and dumb when they'd gotten engaged and their passionate love affair had ended years before she'd come to break it off officially, but that didn't mean I wanted him to spend time alone with her.

Drake came up from the basement and put an arm around Zin. "Ready darling?"

"To meet your father? No," she said with a laugh. "But I suppose it's time." She reached up and pecked a kiss to his lips. "I bet he's as handsome as you but only half as kind."

I let out an audible sigh as Drake's cheeks tinged red.

They were so sweet together and despite the age difference, I was rooting for them. Drake deserved happiness and Zin needed someone to ground her wild edge a bit.

They both gave me hugs then were off to their night and Logan ushered Jasmine upstairs. "Let the damn thing sleep, you can drool over him tomorrow."

"I wasn't drooling, it's the pregnancy hormones," Jasmine insisted but her cheeks were red and she was biting her lower lip.

"Emphasis on the *whore*," Betina shouted from the couch.

"Oh screw you," Annabel shouted back but there was no real vehemence in her words. She grabbed a jar of peanut butter and bag of cookies then headed to the couch. Apparently to eat her desire away.

"What about Evie?" I asked, is she still down there drooling?

"Of course she is, that woman is uncontrollable," Logan said.

I laughed at his scowl. Just the other day Evie had popped into the bathroom when Logan was getting out of the shower. She had no shame for herself, just plenty for other people. "What are we supposed to do when he wakes up and has no idea where the hell he is?" I asked Logan.

"I locked the cell so at least he can't do any damage while he figures it out."

"Oh how comforting for him to wake up in a dark locked cell."

"No options, babe, unless you want to sit down there and wait for the spell to wear off so you can tell him what happened."

I did not think that was a great plan. So we went to bed. I'd deal with the angry accidental prisoner in the morning. Maybe I'd let Annabel explain, he wouldn't stay mad at her.

Chapter Four

The next morning I woke up feeling antsy. I could hear Logan in the shower and I stretched languidly. He would be off to work soon, and I needed to get to the yoga studio. Jasmine and Betina should have gone in early to relieve the night staff so that gave me a little time to be lazy, which I was currently enjoying very much. Last night Logan hadn't let me sleep right away.

I smiled at the memory. Not that I'd minded at all.

I reached over and looked at my cellphone. Zin had sent a message around three this morning to say that Cassius absolutely hated rabbits apparently and he was blaming my whole family for the infestation.

"Great," I grumbled and threw the phone to the blanket. Pumkin howled in distress then jumped from the bed. "Sorry," I whispered to the orange tabby after it was already out the door.

"Who are you apologizing to?" Logan asked from the bathroom.

"Cat."

"How pissed do you think Jason is this morning?"

"Fuck!" I jumped out of bed and scrambled for some sweats. "That's what I was forgetting."

Logan peaked out of the bathroom and grinned. "A night with me and you forget everything else, huh?"

I rolled my eyes. He wasn't wrong, but he didn't need any encouragement in thinking he was good in bed. I pulled on the sweats and a black t-shirt that had little wolves chasing the silhouette of a naked woman all over it. Logan's sister, Lila had given it to me as a joke, but I loved it.

"Finally," Evie said as I stumbled down the stairs, pulling my hair into a quick ponytail.

"Did you at least go talk to him?"

"I did, I explained that you were asleep and would be with him shortly. He knows he isn't your first prisoner and all the others made it out of here alive, though I couldn't guarantee that they survived beyond that."

"Helpful," I grumbled. Jasper and Sofia meowed for food as I hurried through the kitchen. "Be right back," I promised the cats.

Chester swooped in tweeting a good morning and landed on the fridge. He was a bit more patient than the cats. Likely they'd all been fed when Betina and Jasmine were leaving anyway, they just all wanted second breakfast.

"Jason," I called in a friendly tone as I hit the bottom step.

"What is the meaning of this kidnapping?" he demanded. He was standing at the bars to the cell dressed in Logan's jeans, which were a bit too big and hung low on his hips, and a t-shirt that was actually mine and definitely too small riding up over his belly button. He probably had no idea that the clothes weren't supposed to fit like that though and I had a hard time not laughing at the ridiculous picture he made.

"Not kidnapped," I assured him. "You passed out from a spell after Gildar hit you on the boat. We didn't think it safe to dump you back in the water like that," I explained as I unlocked the door.

Jason rubbed his face. "I knew it wasn't just the punch from such a small Elf. He must be a halfling then," Jason looked thoughtful. "Like Annabel."

I wondered if he was debating their compatibility. I could have eased his mind, but it wasn't my job to assure him she wasn't interested in the half Elf, or him. "I didn't want you to freak out when you woke up alone down here, so we locked the cell."

"I want to see Annabel," he demanded, hands on hips and chin notched up. He was obviously used to getting his way and I wondered if he was the leader of the Sirens.

"Of course you do. Come on upstairs and I'll give her a call. Do you like coffee?"

"I don't know."

This should be fun. Another Supe who had spent no time on land was in my care. He followed me upstairs and I poured him a cup of coffee as the cats sniffed his feet.

"What are they?" he asked, looking at them curiously.

"Cats, they are my pets. You smell like fish and they like to eat fish so they are curious to know if they can eat you," I explained, pouring coffee for myself and Logan who would be down any minute.

"Back beasts," he yelled and shook a foot at them.

They didn't move far.

"Here," I said, handing him the cup of coffee and showing him the cream and sugar. He sniffed the black liquid and gagged, then followed my example and poured in a bunch of cream and far too much sugar. He sniffed again and harumphed then took a sip and immediately spit it onto the floor making the cats scatter.

"Sludge," he declared.

"Yep," I agreed and took a large gulp of mine.

"Do you have any squid?"

"Fresh out," I said with a sigh and walked to the freezer. "I might have something frozen..." there was nothing in there except ice cream and toaster waffles. Maybe I needed to start keeping emergency seafood since I was apparently going to harbor sea Supes often enough.

Jason wandered around the house looking at stuff with fascination and Evie popped in to watch him with equal fascination. I messaged Annabel and told her to bring fish food.

She responded with a laughing emoji.

When Logan joined us, I handed him a cup and gave him a kiss. "Annabel's on her way. She'll be dealing with Jason."

"Gildar is out front too," Logan said.

I groaned into my coffee. "Why?"

"I am guessing because he doesn't know where the coven house is, but he knows we have Jason here, so he wants to be sure Annabel doesn't spend time with Jason uninterrupted."

And he knew where I lived because Fanlin had brought him here, lucky me. "Maybe you should take Jason to work with you."

Logan eyed the Siren in question and growled.

"Or Gildar? Tell him you're taking him to Annabel, then just... don't." Seemed like a great idea to me.

"Sorry, I love you, Fawn, but I'm not dealing with either one of Annabel's suitors." With that he left, and I was alone with Jason. Gildar knocked on the door moments later.

With a heavy sigh I opened the front door. "Good morning, Gildar."

"Where is Annabel?"

"Not here. Coffee?" I said and moved so he could come in. No reason to have him standing in front of my house like a creeper. I knew he meant me no harm at least. There was a spell around my house that made it impossible for someone to come in meaning to harm me. My father had installed that without permission before I moved in, but I was very glad he had. I had recently extended it to include Betina too.

"Oh, you're back," Evie said in delight.

"You!" Jason roared and then his voice started to make noises I can't even explain as he weaved a Siren's song to ensnare. It was directed at Gildar though, not me this time, so although I enjoyed the sound, I wasn't panting with the need to throw myself at him and drown happily in his arms.

Gildar was getting the full effect, however. His mouth twisted up into a huge grin and his eyes drooped, he was shuffling across the space toward Jason like he was heading toward his favorite thing.

I had a thought that I should do something, but I couldn't quite make myself. I watched calmly as Gildar walked right up to Jason and Gildar moaned as Jason wrapped his hands around Gildar's neck.

"Stop that, right now," Annabel yelled as she came rushing into the house.

That snapped me out of my funk, and I rushed to help as Annabel tried to wedge herself between the two men.

"I said stop this," she hissed and grabbed Jason's face, forcing him to meet her gaze.

I grabbed Gildar's arm and began to yank him away. It wasn't easy saving someone who didn't want to be saved.

Jason's song cut off and Gildar slumped. Not passed out; but blissed out I'd say by the look on his face. It was really quite creepy. I was not a fan of Sirens, that was for sure.

"Deal with this," I demanded of Jasmine and walked out of the house. I was in charge of a lot, but Annabel's suitor problem was not one of them.

By the time I got to the studio, I was less irritated with Annabel's man trouble, but only because there were so many more rabbits today and that wasn't good, especially in light of Zin's early morning message. It also didn't help that it was again a bright sunny, too hot for October, day. I had too many problems, I couldn't take on Annabel's. I also had no idea where to start with mine technically, so I threw myself into my day job.

"You look, stressed," Betina said brightly when I walked into the studio.

I looked down at myself and sighed. I was in old sweats and my funky t-shirt still. I'd slipped on a pair of flip flops and my hair was in a ponytail that hadn't seen a brush since waking up. I was a Magician and that gave me a natural propensity for flashiness. I didn't usually leave the house looking so haggard, but it seems the last couple of days I'd done nothing but.

"I had to get out of the house," I said and headed for the bathroom, grabbing a bag from my office. I always had extra stuff here to change or freshen up.

When I emerged again, I was feeling good in shiny black yoga shorts and a matching sports bra top. My hair was sleeked into a braid and I'd splashed water on my face.

"Better," Betina offered when I came out.

"Where's Jasmine?"

Betina laughed. "Napping in the empty studio. She stayed up late with me and I made her come in this morning so she's sleeping it off."

"Poor thing, pregnancy must suck," I said. Especially pregnancy alone.

Betina shrugged. "We only needed the one room open this morning anyway, Shaylee called in because she got in an accident last night when it snowed. So I had to cancel half our classes."

"Oh shit! You should have called me. Is she okay?"

"Says she has a bit of whiplash, but other than that she's fine. Her car, not so much. I told her to stay home until she feels good enough to work and not to worry about anything."

I nodded and frowned, I couldn't help feeling like this was my fault, though indirectly. I needed to figure out this weather thing before more people got hurt. "Do what you can to fill in her schedule and let me know what classes I need to pick up."

"Will do boss," she said with a wink.

I headed in to teach a class that was about to start, then taught a couple more. There was no better way for me to relax and sometimes it even helped me come up with solutions. Today though, I was coming up empty class after class. My body was relaxed but my mind was reeling. I caught up on paperwork when our afternoon teachers came in, Jasmine and Betina were already gone for the day, and before I knew it, it was almost sunset again. Cassius would be up soon, apparently demanding solutions. I had nothing to tell Zin.

I pulled out my phone and texted my father. His response was firmly in the; we have no information, but we better figure it the fuck out, category.

"Great," I grumbled and shoved the phone into my bag.

As I looked out the window and glared at the rabbits between the front door and my car, the sky started to rapidly darken and snowflakes drifted down. Within five minutes the rabbits were gone but there were at least three inches of snow on the ground.

"Again?" Sam groaned as she stopped to put on her sweater. Sam was my long-time human employee and I relied on her to run the place a lot of the time. She had no idea me and so many of the other girls were not so human, but sometimes I wondered if she questioned it. She'd been around since before I started going twenty-four hours and anyone who met Zin had to wonder about her. She was just a little bit too much to be real. It's one of the things I loved about her.

"Drive careful," I said and held the door for her.

I stared for a few more minutes and watched it come down. I may claim to be a P.I. for the supernatural, but this felt way beyond my abilities. I didn't have any high-tech gear to analyze weather patterns or tiny microchips to follow rabbits around. It was just me and a few helpful friends hoping to get a lucky break. I felt like a fraud and all I wanted to do was help people.

Chapter Five

By the time I got home, far slower than usual, the snow had dumped five inches in forty-five minutes and the evening was again clear and cool like a normal October. Arguably clearer than normal.

It felt like someone was flipping a switch on and off and probably laughing their assess off while they watched us all squeal and squirm.

"He fucked up this time," Betina shouted when I walked into the house. She was dancing in front of the television and I could see the news behind her. Evie was of course glued to it too, as it was her favorite werewolf anchor talking about the snow. Tony was on the couch watching her excitement with a grin, Pumpkin purring in his lap.

Annabel was hovering with interested eyes on the television but neither of her suitors were in sight and that was a relief. Then I heard the bathroom door open and out walked Jason. A sharp hiss in the kitchen told me where the other one was. How she'd gotten them to not fight, I had no idea, but it felt like a sort of peace had settled over the group.

Chester tweeted a greeting and landed on my shoulder. No dogs rushed forward to greet me and my heart ached for their loss still. Even with all the people and the cats and a bird, it was still too quiet in my opinion.

"Who fucked up? And how?" I asked.

"This weather shit, look at that pattern!" Betina squealed again. "Logan and Jasmine are already on their way to check it out, storm knocked out a cell tower so they couldn't call you."

"Logan and Jasmine went together?" Worry tightened my chest, this wasn't good.

"I would have gone too, but Tweedle Dee and Tweedle Dumb wouldn't stay behind and Logan banned them from riding with him," Annabel explained.

That made sense but it didn't relieve the tension in my stomach at the thought of those two alone. Logan would never harm a pregnant woman, but she might hurt *him* if he got too mouthy which he definitely had a tendency to do when he didn't like someone. Jasmine had the ability to produce a very large electric shock from her fingers and she'd be able to knock his ass out with a touch I was pretty sure. "How did they know where to go?"

"The snow laid out in a perfect circle," Betina said, waving at the television. "The center has to be where the guy is; or was anyway."

Finally, a place to start. I could feel my anxiety start to fade. If I was actively trying to solve it, then I had no reason to feel guilty. I just hoped Cassius would agree.

"It's weather, what are you all carrying on about?" Evie waved at us dramatically and popped out. Never one to get involved in supernatural affairs.

I checked my cell, it was still dead. "Well let's see if we can get there and help before they're done figuring it out."

"I'll drive," Annabel offered. Which was the cue for Gildar and Jason to race out of the house, presumably to get the passenger seat first.

I was glad to see someone had gotten Jason one of Logan's shirts, though he was still wearing the too big pants, he didn't look ridiculous now, he just looked deliciously baggy. "How did you manage to keep them from killing each other?"

"I told them that if they pulled anything like that again I was going to kill them both. They didn't believe me, but when I said that I would definitely not want to be with the one who hurt the other, they decided to start playing nice and now they're almost more annoying."

I laughed even as I felt sorry for my friend. "Maybe you can convince Fanlin to come get Gildar since a day with him didn't convince you that you're soulmates."

"I already tried. He said not until this whole thing is resolved. He's definitely using it as an excuse, I don't think he's actually concerned for my safety. Jason says he's committed to staying up on land until then too because he needs to report back that things were resolved." She looked at me with narrowed eyes. "Another excuse. So I just hope we can make this a one night and done situation."

I doubted we would. "Maybe you'll fall in love while we solve this shit," I suggested, and she glared daggers at me.

Betina thought it was funny, letting out a laugh and I think Tony hid his laugh under a cough. I ran upstairs to change before Annabel could decide to curse me.

I needed to change anyway, no way was I traipsing through the snow in flipflops and sweats.

Annabel's SUV was better in the snow than my cute little sports car, so we made decent time as we headed to the Space Needle a few minutes later. It was the center of the weather phenomenon from what we could tell on the weather report. Jason had won the spot beside Annabel up front, Gildar sat behind her leaning forward so he was practically sharing her seat no matter how many times she swatted back at him and demanded he sit back or she'd crash deliberately. The rest of us filled in without complaint. Tony and Betina cuddled in the very back and I was in the seat next to Gildar.

"I hope we catch the asshole, I am not a winter Troll," Betina complained, and Tony put his arm around her. Instantly the car warmed up by about five degrees. He was a handy little Warlock for a cold day. Betina giggled and I could see Annabel roll her eyes in the rearview mirror.

Unfortunately we weren't the only ones who'd noticed the pattern center. Or whoever was to blame had tripped some kind of alarm on the Needle, dragging the cops into our business. We parked as close as we could and still had to walk a few blocks to get near the Needle, making me regret my footwear choice. These boots were adorable with my black skinny jeans and though they were better than flipflops, I discovered on the walk from house to car that they leaked water like mad and my socks were now soggy.

By the time we got close to the Space Needle it was surrounded by Police and news reporters. Curious spectators had gathered around it too, drawn by the cameras and official activity.

"Damnit, he's made an obvious show of himself. He's fucking up and humans are going to start asking questions that can't be safely answered, I hissed as we circled, trying to find a spot close to park.

When we found a spot, not exactly a legal spot but a spot all the same, our group hustled to the crowd, and I frowned. Any evidence we might have been able to gather was gone, trampled by a hundred different scents and pairs of feet.

"Ms. Malero, I'm glad to see you're here looking into this," a voice said as we pushed through the crowd.

A few curious human faces turned my way.

I turned to glare at whoever had spoken. As far as any human knew, I was a business owner and nothing more. Good at yoga and that was it. I was surprised to see a somewhat familiar Vampire face looking at me with a raised eyebrow over ice blue eyes, his mouth quirked just enough to hint at the fangs underneath. If that wasn't enough to tell me Vamp, he was dressed in a timeless sort of style of black slacks and button up shirt with a wool coat over his shoulders. He looked sleek and dangerous, but not obvious.

"I'm sorry, Do I know you?" I couldn't place the man.

"I work the bar downtown," the man said with a laugh. "We've never officially met, but I've served you a cup of wine or two." He held out his hand. "Saul."

"Nice to officially meet you, Saul." I did recognize him then. A nice bartender at the local Vamp club. I felt a bit of shame color my cheeks realizing I'd never cared to learn the man's name. "I am here to see what's up, but I don't even know for sure if it's a Supe," I whispered the last but I knew he'd catch it.

"As if it would be anything else before the big wedding. Probably someone trying to cause trouble for the powerful couple," he whispered back.

"I hope not." That would put Cassius way too far into my business if it was.

"Dante is a formidable vampire, as you know well. His father even more so. They both have enemies and some aren't happy about the choice of grooms. Whoever marries young Anthea will be an important part of a powerful family."

Heat filled my body as I thought about Dante. Never in my life had I been so attracted to a Vampire, but it wasn't my fault, the damn fanger had invaded my mind, my dreams, and my life. I'd happily sent him on his way without ever giving in to more than a kiss, but he was coming back, and I wasn't sure how I felt about that.

Saul cleared his throat, and I realized I was touching my lips. I dropped my hand and glared at him, hoping to hell that he wasn't able to read minds or some shit.

"It's possible, but hopefully not. I assure you we are working on it either way. What are people here saying?" I asked.

"Not much, the humans are confused and mostly convinced it's an evil scientist or God punishing them. The Supes are worried it's an evil scientist or Supe with a God complex." He shrugged.

"My money is on God complex," I said.

Annabel leaned in beside me. "This is probably an evil Magician. Or an evil Magician's toy."

"Not a Troll, we don't go in for death and destruction, we are harmonious with nature," Betina pointed out.

"Which leads us back to Supe with a God complex," Saul said with a sigh. "I'm off to work, good luck Ms. Malero, we're all counting on you to keep the city safe." He bowed slightly and hurried off, blending quickly with the shadows.

"No pressure," I mumbled.

We moved forward into the crowd and pushed toward the police line. It wasn't hard to spot Logan among the crowd there. He had a presence about him that drew me like nothing else and I felt something inside me settle as I laid eyes on him. He was my man and he made me feel whole after years of not belonging.

Logan turned when I approached, his dark eyes seeking me out immediately. He moved through the people and brought me in for a tight hug. "Fawn, love, what took you so long?"

"My car doesn't like the snow," I said with a laugh.

"And neither does my Magician, does she?" Logan said and leaned down for a quick kiss.

"This is exciting," Jasmine said brightly, having followed Logan through the crowd. "I heard more than one Supe murmuring about you. They think you'll handle this, you're definitely making a name for yourself, Fawn."

Pressure, I thought to myself. "Is there any evidence left to follow?" I pulled away from Logan and looked at my friend, Logan kept a possessive arm around my back.

"We have an insider," she whispered conspiratorially.

I quirked an eyebrow up at Logan.

"Brandon is out there with the police, he'll let us know if they find anything useful. So far, they're just talking about meteorological phenomena and vandals trying to break into the Needle. I think they've got the news guys looking into it, but they don't really know anything either. Someone mentioned calling NASA," Logan explained.

Brandon was a Werewolf in Logan's pack and that was comforting, hopefully he could keep them from calling NASA just yet. The more humans involved would only make it harder for us to find any supernatural evidence. There were a few Werewolves and Magicians in key positions throughout the city that helped make things go smoothly for us. Despite our best efforts, sometimes people fucked up.

I'd fucked up on my first mission, leaving behind evidence in a human's basement. I knew better now, but still, backup plans were always a good thing.

"Hey, do you think someone's trying to ruin Anthea's wedding?" I asked.

Logan looked like he was seriously considering it as an option. "No, I think if someone didn't want Anthea's marriage to happen, they'd be doing something to the groom or bride themselves, probably the groom. Attacking Seattle, especially since they aren't even here yet, wouldn't make any sense."

"Cassius is here, maybe it's about him?"

Logan shrugged. "Could be, but I still doubt it. This doesn't feel targeted, this feels like an attack on the entire city."

I agreed, but it was nice to get a second opinion. That left no leads as to why though, and maybe no leads as to who, unless something came up here tonight.

"So we wait, or what?" Annabel asked, obviously disappointed that we weren't hot on the trail to anything. We were also all standing in snow and not really dressed for it. Luckily Annabel was wearing leather pants, but I was sure she had wet feet too. Logan wouldn't be bothered; Werewolves ran hot. But Jasmine was pregnant and dressed in tennis shoes and yoga pants. She had to be freezing. Betina looked like she couldn't care less, wrapped in Tony's warm embrace. Jason and Gildar were too busy jockeying for a position close to Annabel to notice or care about the weather. They were also getting a lot of looks from the crowd around them which wasn't good. Someone was going to notice something off about them and then we'd have rumors floating around.

"How about us girls take Jasmine home, maybe you men can wait for word from Brandon and check out the crowd some more?" I suggested.

Tony looked disappointed but nodded. Jason and Gildar were emphatically disagreeing. They both swore they had to stay near Annabel and keep her safe.

"No, I want you two to figure this shit out," Annabel said sternly. "Stay, stay with Logan," Annabel demanded, treating them a bit like naughty puppies and it made me laugh.

"I'll sniff around, maybe I can pick up something nearby," Logan said.

"I'll crowd surf," Tony said. "If anyone here has touched magic lately, I might catch a sense of it." Tony kissed Betina before disappearing into the crowd of mostly humans.

I kissed Logan and grabbed Jasmine's arm. Annabel gave Gildar and Jason scolding looks, then walked away. They watched her go with matching looks of dejection. Jasmine and I followed Annabel.

"I bet I can find something great," Jason said when Annabel was through the crowd, and I heard Gildar huff. Well at least they were motivated to help.

When we were far enough away that I was sure Logan couldn't hear, I asked Jasmine if he'd been nice.

She laughed. "He's grumpy as usual, but yes, I think he's starting to understand that I am not here to steal you away."

The look she gave me made me wonder if she would if she thought I could be swayed.

I looked away and gave her arm a squeeze. "How's the baby today?"

"Exhausting," she said with a laugh. "I took multiple naps and I'm starving again."

"I think we have waffles and ice cream at home," I offered, and she gave me a bright smile. Maybe because I'd called it home and not *my house*. She was welcome as long as she needed, her and the little bundle in her belly.

By the time we were settled back at the house, the snow was half melted and Betina had informed me that there were again rabbits hopping around in the yard. I scowled at my cats. They should go chase them away. At least Jasper had swiped at the one trying to poke its head in the cat door earlier. The dogs would have happily chased them out of the yard, but then I would have felt bad for the rabbits, so maybe it was good that the cats left them mostly alone. Jasper and Sophia were now cuddled up and cleaning each other on the couch while Pumpkin purred on Jasmine's lap. It was a happy scene.

"Your baby is going to come out purring," I teased.

She smiled and stroked the cat. "Better than coming out screaming, I guess." She patted her still flat stomach. "Safe and happy are the two most important things though, and I'm working on it." She sighed heavily.

I sat beside her and put an arm around her shoulder. "You know I'll do whatever I can to make that happen, Jasmine."

She looked at me with eyes glistening unshed tears. "He contacted me again. Sent a messenger this time. I think he's in the city Fawn, and I'm scared."

Protectiveness boiled inside me. How dare he come to my city and make someone feel unsafe. "What did he say?"

She pulled a note from her pocket and handed it to me.

Wife-

I expect this nonsense to end. Call me.

-Maddox, your husband.

"Wow, straight and to the point."

"Yeah, I don't know, maybe I should call him, maybe I can make him understand..." she trailed off as if she didn't even believe the words that she was saying.

"Maybe we should send Logan and his pack to *talk* to him," Betina shouted from the kitchen, obviously already having read the note. She was probably home when it had arrived, and I would have been angry at her for not telling me, but I supposed with the other things going on in the city it had slipped her mind.

"Don't call him," I ordered. "If he's in town he'll show his face, and when he does you won't be alone." I grabbed her hand and smiled reassuringly. I'd make sure Jasmine wasn't left alone until this was solved. There was no way Maddox was going to harm her with witnesses.

"I can get my coven to work a spell, make him want to leave the city," Annabel offered.

Jasmine just shook her head. "No, I need to deal with him permanently. I just don't know how. If we use magic, he'll eventually come back. I need him to really understand that it is over."

I couldn't argue with that, although I really liked Annabel's suggestion. We settled in with popcorn and a movie. Evie hovered and I was surprised she wasn't putting in her two cents on the subject. I'd expect her to be of the opinion that a woman needed to stay with the father of her children.

Her silence made me like her a little bit more.

The men arrived a while later looking frustrated. Jason and Gildar both immediately moved to stand near Annabel.

"Did you find anything?" I asked hopefully.

Tony shook his head. "No one smelled like magic that powerful."

"Brandon said he could smell magic around the Space Needle when they had first arrived, but other than that, nothing. Too many other scents to pinpoint one to follow."

"Damn," Betina grumbled.

We were back to nothing.

"We need a motive," Jasmine pointed out and we all looked at her because she was right, and it didn't help at all either.

"Alright, come on Gildar," Tony said. "You're staying with me again I assume?"

"Thank you," I said.

"No, I am staying with Annabel," Gildar said.

"No, I am staying with Annabel," Jason stated.

"No one is staying with Annabel," Annabel hissed. "Jason, go home. Gildar, go back to the Elf clan."

"But we shared a magical time," Jason insisted and grasped Annabel's arms. "I declared my love for you and sang you the song of love as I entered—"

"Stop!" Annabel shouted and pulled away from him. "Just stop."

Jason looked shocked then horribly saddened and shuffled his feet. "You do not love me," he whispered.

"No, I don't," she stated firmly.

"You wish to become this half Elf's wife?" Jason added and Gildar brightened, puffing out his chest.

"No, I wish to be left alone." Annabel's words were so full of frustration it pulled at my instincts to help.

"Typical Witch," Betina said. I shot her a glare and she just shrugged, she wasn't wrong.

"Then I will stay, I will prove that I am a good choice," Jason declared.

Annabel looked at me pleadingly, but I had nothing to offer. I thought she was being clear with her desires toward them, they were just being ridiculous. I looked at Logan for help.

Logan took a deep breath. "Okay, boys, here's how things go. You take no for an answer. That's the end of it. Jason, go with Tony and hop on into the sound. Gildar, you go with Tony and call up Fanlin, you're not needed here anymore. Got it?" He used his alpha voice, calm but commanding and even I got a tingle to obey.

Gildar and Jason both looked from him to Annabel.

"This is what you want, truly?" Gildar asked.

"Yes," Annabel said, throwing up her hands in frustration. "If I change my mind, I'll call you."

"I will await your call," Jason said and stripped out of his clothes. "I am ready to return to my home and wait."

We all just stared at the now naked man.

Evie fanned herself but didn't look away from Jason.

"Christ," Tony mumbled, "No naked asses on my car seats. Let's go." He kissed Betina and walked out of the house.

"Until then," Jason said and touched Annabel's cheek then followed Tony out ignoring the comment about his nudity.

Hopefully Tony had a towel in the car or something.

"My father will be disappointed," Gildar said sadly.

"So will mine apparently," Annabel said.

"I will anxiously await your change of mind. Be safe, Annabel."

Annabel waved him out and he followed slowly.

When the door shut behind Gildar, we all sighed in relief.

"You have to admit, that Jason is packing heat," Jasmine said, breaking the silence.

"That man is a god," Evie agreed.

Logan grunted and headed upstairs. Annabel rolled her eyes, "You two can have him."

"Ha! Who wants a pregnant married mess like this," Jasmine said. She was trying to joke but I felt the pain in that statement. She felt unwanted and she worried she'd always be that way.

"If I was ten years younger," Evie said.

"More like a hundred," I said and she sniffed and disappeared.

I gave Jasmine a hug from behind the couch. "You don't want Jason, I heard what he does during sex," I laughed.

"Oh do tell," Jasmine said brightly, her mood suddenly quite improved. That's one thing I'd always loved about Jasmine, nothing kept her down for long.

"No thanks, I lived it. I'll see you guys tomorrow I'm sure," Annabel said and left.

"Are we eating ice cream and watching Dirty Dancing again?" Betina asked Jasmine.

"Of course we are, and I'll try to stay awake through the whole thing," Jasmine said.

"Goodnight girls," I called and went up to join Logan in the bedroom.

That night when I was curled up in Logan's arms, I told him about Jasmine's latest message from Maddox and how I wanted to make doubly sure she was never alone.

"I can't argue with that. I guess that means we need to bring her to Brakemoor with us."

I bit my lip and ran a hand over his chest. Maybe I could distract him from arguing with me about it. "I was thinking I'd stay behind during the full moon to watch her." My hand had traveled all the way south and he was glaring at me and my obvious attempt to win the coming argument.

"Fawn," he hissed in a breath as I squeezed gently. "This is my first full moon run as Alpha, I want you by my side."

"Do you also want Jasmine there, because I don't feel like I can leave her alone in the city." I punctuated my words with kisses along his chest making him groan.

"You're a vixen, Fawn."

I smiled up at him, knowing he wasn't going to disagree.

"Bring her to Brakemoor if you must, I won't have my pack thinking you choose any duty over them."

He pulled me roughly to him, distracting me from the thoughts that statement brought up and kissed me deeply. For a time I thought of nothing other than how he could play my body perfectly.

When I lay sated in his arms though, my mind began to circle those words. His pack over any other duty? Was that what they expected of me? Could I really promise that?

I knew that I wouldn't miss a full moon with Logan if I could help it. And it felt good to know he wanted me there, but I wouldn't leave behind an innocent in need for it. I wouldn't choose going to Brakemoor to stand around while they ran off into the woods over helping someone who needs me here.

I wasn't a Werewolf, I was a Magician, and my priorities would always be my duty to the city and its supernaturals. Maybe I was more like my father than I realized.

Logan's snores accompanied my brooding thoughts. I loved him deeply, but he was Werewolf alpha and his priorities would always be the pack above all else.

Were we doomed?

Chapter Six

The next day was hotter than it should have been, the snow was completely gone, and the rabbits were back in force. I stared out the window drinking my third cup of coffee and debating my options.

"It feels like biblical plague levels around here. Rabbits instead of locust, the storms instead of drought, next comes what? Famine or disease?" Jasmine asked from the couch as she sipped her tea.

"I'm guessing disease, seeing as they keep pooping on the sidewalk, that can't be healthy. Can rabbits carry the black plague?" I've had to wash more than one pair of shoes because of the feces. "The heat really gets it stinking too," I mock gagged. If it was normal fall cool, then it wouldn't be nearly as bad. The one good thing was whenever we got the freak snowstorms that melted off, it washed some of it away.

Even still, the city was working overtime trying to sweep streets and even started paying some homeless to go around poop scooping. The whole thing had made it onto the national news this morning and my father was starting to receive calls from Supes outside our city asking what the hell was going on. Which had prompted him to send texts to me and my brothers saying we had to all step up our investigations.

Unfortunately, none of the Magicians in other cities who called had any insight as to why or how or what to do. I think they were just calling to annoy my father who had been successfully running this city for a hundred years. I just couldn't prove it was supernatural, the damn things wouldn't talk to me. Of course that might be sign enough that it *was* supernatural because animals had never refused to talk to me before.

The weather was starting to make the rounds nationally too, but so far no one was calling my father about that, at least no one that wasn't in the city. No one had died from either issue that I knew of, so what was the point of all of this? If someone was sending in the rabbits, what were they hoping to accomplish? Obviously someone was deliberately messing with the weather, but what was the point of that? What motive was there for either? It was like being annoyed to death by a little brother. They weren't going to get grounded for it, but if you reacted and punched them in the face you would be sitting in the corner with your nose to the wall.

Was someone trying to mess with us? Hoping for an overreaction that we would be punished for? I had to be careful, and I had to figure it out sooner rather than later. Which made taking a couple days' vacation to Brakemoor sound like a really bad idea.

"How about this for the wedding?" Betina asked as she strode into the room, breaking me from my thoughts. She was wearing a floor length black dress with a slit up to her thigh and a conservative neckline. When she spun, I saw how far the dress dipped in the back, not conservative but completely gorgeous.

"You look beautiful, Betina, is Tony going to come too, someone is going to have to keep the other men off you," I said.

She beamed at my praise. "Yeah, he's going to look like a super hottie in a tux, I can't wait!"

"Oh I love weddings," Evie said with a sigh and popped out. I had a feeling next time we saw her she'd be in a wedding gown, she got pretty reminiscent from time to time.

"I need a dress." Unless Logan was too mad at me to let me attend with him, because as I watched a car swerve around a cluster of rabbits in the middle of the street, I knew I had to be working on the problems here. No matter what his duties to the pack were. I couldn't go with him to Brakemoor, no way.

"Rex asked me to go as his plus one," Jasmine said, and I gave her a shocked look. Her face heated with embarrassment. "I figured why not, it will be a fun party and for now at least, I don't look pregnant. Who knows when I'll get a chance to feel pretty in a nice dress again."

I couldn't argue with that.

"When did you see Rex?" My oldest brother was the least happy about my position in the city and never visited unless he was here to yell at me for something. He was slowly taking over for my father so it was no surprise that he would attend the wedding as official representative for the Seattle Magicians. I guess I just expected him to go alone.

"I didn't, he just messaged me this morning and asked. Is that okay?" She looked suddenly worried.

"Fine, if you want to hang out with his lame ass," I laughed. "I'll be glad to have another friend in the crowd of Vamps."

"I guess we need to go shopping then." I turned back to the yard and watched a particularly large white rabbit hop by. "I wonder how the rest of the Vampires feel about rabbits." I knew Cassius wasn't a fan. I also wondered how the city was going to deal with the influx of so many Vampires. This wedding was going to be a huge affair drawing Vampires in from all around the world.

Evie popped in then, wearing a lace wedding gown that I knew had been hers. I'd seen pictures of her on her wedding day. She'd been a beautiful young bride with a handsome husband. The looks on their faces had been pure joy, not a care in the world and no doubts about the life they wanted to lead together.

I wanted that someday and I wanted it forever after. I didn't want to make mistakes and end up... well end up like Jasmine.

Last time I'd been at Brakemoor, when Logan had accepted his place as Alpha, his mother had basically stuck an engagement ring on me by giving me a choker she'd worn when Logan's father had become Alpha. Most of the pack probably considered it a done deal aside from the official ceremony. I think Logan did too, though he'd not gone on one knee and asked me.

We'd talked vaguely about the future; someday, marriage, kids, the whole deal. But in this moment looking at Evie and knowing what kind of love she'd had in her short human life; I wondered if I was making a mistake.

Should love ask you to give up what was most important to you? Logan wanted me to choose the full moon run over my job, my calling, my duty.

"I wore red at my wedding," Jasmine said with a laugh. "Maybe that was a sign that it wasn't going to last."

"Red!" Evie scoffed, horrified.

"Oh yes. Maddox wore a white suit, and I wore a red gown. It was gorgeous, I didn't want to pretend I was a blushing virgin," she said with a smile. "I thought red would better signify the passion we had for each other and the reason we wanted to be together. Not just a good match politically, but also we were dynamite in bed."

"A necessity to a good marriage," Evie agreed, surprising me.

"Damn, Evie, gross," Betina said with a mock gag.

"Passion isn't bound by age, Betina," Evie huffed.

"Or death apparently," Jasmine snarked.

Passion was something Logan and I definitely had. I clung to that thought as I rinsed my coffee mug and picked up my cell. I needed to let him know that I had too many duties here, I couldn't pack up and leave tonight, I just couldn't! I also couldn't text him. I was a chicken shit, so I thumped up the stairs to get dressed instead. Maybe I could solve a problem today and feel alright about leaving town.

"Who wants to catch rabbits with me today?" I yelled as I walked into my room.

Silence met me. That was fine, I needed alone time to think.

Thirty rabbits and a trip to the outskirts of the city and back later, I found myself sitting in my car in my garage. No closer to knowing how to handle things.

My decision was made for me when I heard yelling in the house. I rushed in through the garage door and to the front door where Betina was yelling at a very large man who had to be Maddox by the look of horror and tears on Jasmine's face.

"Get out of here, you asshole!" Betina was threatening and the smell of rotten fish filled the space around her.

"Shit, woman," Maddox gagged and stepped back, covering his face. He had long white hair with a streak of dyed red near his ear giving him a punk sort of look that went well with his eyeliner and pierced eyebrow. His features were sharp but not unattractive and his black eyes were intense as they looked from Betina to me. "I demand to speak to my wife."

"She doesn't want to *be* your wife anymore. Take a hint," Betina yelled.

"Fuck that, she's carrying my child and we have an agreement."

"Not anymore," Betina hissed and slammed the door in his face.

"Oh god," Jasmine gasped and grabbed her stomach, then ran for the bathroom. Moments later the sound of puking followed.

"I think that was your fault," I pointed out and opened the kitchen window.

"Yeah well, it got him to back up enough to shut the door," she defended. "He rushed inside before I knew who it was."

"Who's the hottie on the front lawn?" Evie asked, popping in with a bright smile.

"Jasmine's husband, we don't like him," Betina pointed out.

"Oh, well the child will no doubt be gorgeous with them as parents," Evie said, she was still in her wedding dress.

"I'll go talk to him." I walked outside. Betina stood in the open door, arms crossed over her chest and glaring.

He couldn't hurt me as long as I was on my property so Betina stayed back to guard Jasmine.

"She carries my child," Maddox snapped.

"She doesn't want to be in a relationship with you, child or not."

Maddox fisted his hands at his sides and narrowed his eyes at me.

"You're the bitch she's been in love with huh, she ran back to you at the first chance she got. She stole my seed and now she thinks she can have it all!" His words exploded out of him, and I felt a small tremble beneath my feet.

I took a step back. This was a powerful Magician. "Get a lawyer, Maddox, divorce and a custody agreement, that's the way these things go."

He reached out and grabbed my arm, fear sliced through me, and the smell of Betina's Troll defense wrapped around us as she moved to stand right behind me.

"Let go," Betina said darkly.

I reached for my pepper spray or stun gun but both were in my purse in the car. Damnit, I hated when I did that. I needed to strap the things to my belt.

"Damnit Maddox, don't hurt her!" Jasmine cried from the porch and rushed out onto the lawn. Betina grabbed her so she wouldn't get close enough for him to grab.

"You'll come back to me," he demanded, not letting go of me.

"No, I won't," she snapped. "I'm done with your abuse, your controlling demands. I want a life of my own and I won't let you or my father tell me what to do anymore."

"And this little whore is what you want?" He hissed, shaking me slightly.

The squeal of tires and slam of a door stopped any more conversation.

"Get your hands off of her," Logan growled as he stalked across the yard. His eyes were narrowed onto Maddox. His body rippled slightly and I knew he'd change instantly if he thought I was in serious danger. I didn't want that to happen, but I also didn't like being grabbed by an angry Magician. How had he managed to assault me even this much on my property?

"What business is it of yours, Wolf," Maddox demanded, but he did let my arm go.

I hurried to Jasmine's other side, putting a comforting arm around her as she shuddered with fear. This stress couldn't be good for the baby. The overwhelming smell of Betina's defense wasn't good for any of us. "Fuck, Betina tamp it down now, will you?" I whispered as bile started to rise up my throat.

"Saved your damn life, but whatever," she grumped, but the air started to clear as the two males glared at each other.

"She is my mate, and you will *not* touch her again," Logan growled.

Maddox glanced at me with surprise, then back to Logan. "Is she, then why is *my* whore of a wife trying to set up house with her?"

"None of your damn business," Logan snarled. "Neither of those women are your business. In fact if I see you around here again, I will take a chunk out of you to remind you who's city you're in."

The threat was real, and I could see a flash of fear in Maddox's eyes before he shook his head and notched his chin high.

"That is my child, my wife by law, and I won't be kept from either."

"Consider your divorce final. As far as the child; prove it," Logan snapped, not backing down an inch.

Maddox shot a promising glare at Jasmine, then hurried off. I had no doubt we'd see him again.

Jasmine rushed across the yard to embrace Logan. Tears streaming down her face as she thanked him over and over.

Love for that man filled me and tears stung my own eyes. He'd just defended Jasmine and basically claimed her as his own against Maddox. He could have just as easily taken Maddox's side, could have seen this as the opportunity to get rid of a problem between us.

Damn if I wasn't weak-kneed for that kind of domineering care.

I walked over to him and kissed him as Jasmine slipped away looking embarrassed. "Thank you," I whispered against his lips.

"You are my mate, and I'll take care of everyone in your family. I know Jasmine matters to you, I'll protect her the same as I would Betina or Annabel," he whispered back.

Fuck, I was lost to this Werewolf.

"Everyone pack up, we're heading to Brakemoor," I called out as I stared up into Logan's eyes.

"I thought you were going to leave me hanging," he said.

"Never," I said with a wink.

"Why didn't the wards work? He should have been compelled out of your yard as soon as his thoughts turned to harming you," Logan said with concern.

He was right, I looked around in confusion until I saw a small crack in the walkway. "His little earthquake was enough to break the circle." I looked at Logan with worry. Maddox was dangerous.

Chapter Seven

The drive to Brakemoor was long and filled with stops so Logan could eat and eat. He always consumed a lot, but before a full moon he was insatiable. It worked well for the pregnant lady though; she enjoyed snacking often too, and she had to pee a lot.

Betina had decided to stay behind and cat sit she said. I knew she was really going to enjoy alone time with Tony, I couldn't blame her. Alone was hard to get lately. It had been surprisingly easy to convince Jasmine to go with us, she was always up for an adventure, that hadn't changed in all these years. It was harder to tell my father I'd be out of town for a couple days but promised to come back ready to investigate all the troubles. He reminded me I had a duty to the city, and I reminded him that technically I only had a duty to a small portion of the city and Rex was training to be in charge of the entire thing.

Then I got a text from Rex saying I was a brat. I could live with that.

What if Logan was my happily ever after? What if we had little babies that would wolf out once a month and need to run with the pack? I didn't want the pack to think I wasn't good enough for Logan, and part of that was embracing this part of his life as part of my own. The same way he'd embraced Jasmine as part of his. All it had taken was a visible threat and his alpha need to protect the weak was on high alert.

We arrived at the lodge in the middle of the night but Logan's mother, Silvara and his sister, Lila, were up to greet us with hugs and smiles. Silvara fussed over Jasmine, Logan having filled her in on the situation before we'd left the city.

When she hugged me, she whispered, "Thank you for coming, I know it's not the best time." in my ear and I felt bad for ever considering not attending. I knew how important this was for Logan and his entire pack. How hard this particular full moon would be without Samuel. Silvara had to be in a lot of pain right now, but she was keeping it together so well. If I didn't know she'd just lost her husband and oldest son, I would think everything was as it always had been.

"I wouldn't want to be anywhere else," I assured her.

Logan gave me a soft smile as Silvara showed Jasmine to a guest room.

"So he showed up and threatened you?" Lila asked when Silvara and Jasmine were out of the room.

"Yeah, Logan rushed up to claim her right away," I said happily. "He's a good man." I watched him from the window with a grin, as he grabbed our bags out of the truck.

"He's alright," Lila said with a wink. She loved her big brother but couldn't miss a chance to give him a hard time. "Are you ready for tomorrow?"

"What do you mean?" I asked carefully, wondering what Logan hadn't told me.

"Well I think everyone is coming. It's going to be a packed house. They all want to meet you, if they haven't already, the Magician vixen who stole the alpha's heart."

"Yikes, no pressure," I grumbled.

Lila gave me a side hug. "Don't worry, they are all glad to know Logan is happy and in charge. They are just curious about you for obvious reasons."

I wasn't sure I knew it was so obvious.

"See you tomorrow," Logan said to his sister and ushered me up to his room. It was a beautiful room in a beautiful lodge. Logan was good with his hands, and he'd built a lot of the furniture here. I loved sleeping in the big bed surrounded by his handywork, it made me feel safe and he was always extra frisky when we were in it which was a big win in my opinion.

The next morning, I woke alone in the big bed which wasn't surprising. Logan had a lot of extra duties now that he was alpha and I could already hear a lot of activity downstairs. Wolves had started arriving for tonight's celebration.

I didn't rush as I got dressed in jeans and a light sweater that hugged my body and made me feel a little sexy. I left my hair loose around my shoulders and put on enough makeup and jewelry to feel dressed up in a casual way. A Magician rarely went around looking casual.

Then I went downstairs to find Jasmine and coffee. Jasmine was in the kitchen with Lila eating breakfast and giggling at something out the back windows.

"What is it?" I asked and hurried to see what the two women were staring at.

I was treated to the sight of a couple of naked men walking from the tree line to a cabin following one naked female.

"I think they're celebrating early," Lila said with a laugh.

The full moon made all the Werewolves extra frisky and none of them cared much about walking around nude here, so the sight wasn't unusual, but Jasmine was new to all this and found it very interesting.

"Coffee?" Lila asked and handed me a cup.

I took it thankfully and settled in at the counter, facing away from the windows. I had no interest in seeing more of these people naked.

"Did you sleep well?" I asked Jasmine.

"So well. I knew that there was no way Maddox was showing up here," she sighed. "I haven't slept that well in years."

I tried not to take offense. She should feel just as safe at my house but maybe she hadn't thought Logan would truly defend her against Maddox before yesterday. Maybe that's why she stayed up late with Betina every night despite the early mornings. She couldn't fall asleep until she was exhausted enough to pass out. Hopefully she wouldn't have any trouble sleeping from here on out.

Throughout the day, more and more wolves arrived. It was a large pack and although most full moons didn't bring everyone to Brakemoor, this was a special occasion that warranted more than usual.

The men treated me with respect and the women, well, if they were mated they did too, but more than one unmated female gave me side-eye and I was thankful for Jasmine because she never missed an opportunity to talk loudly about how disgustingly in love Logan and I were and how it made her so jealous of a good relationship in the last few weeks she'd been at my place. It made Lila laugh every time and my face turned red every time.

Logan spent the day holed up in what was now *his* office dealing with pack matters. Everyone who had a complaint or need got their time with him and I hadn't seen him all day.

"Has he even eaten?" I asked Silvara well after lunch.

"I made sure he got coffee and breakfast, but that was pretty early, and he hasn't been out of there since. The pack is testing him, making sure he's got the loyalty and stamina to be alpha," she said conspiratorially.

That made sense, at least they weren't challenging him physically. I knew that was a possibility all alphas dealt with. Any other Wolf could challenge them for their position at any time and although it didn't happen too often, it was a fear I was going to have to live with. If he was respected, no one would challenge his position and that's what he was working on now, I supposed. Showing that he was all in and it was my job as his... partner? Mate?... to support him in that.

So I took the plate Silvara handed me and walked toward the office with confidence. I could feel every eye on me as I went and whispers so quiet even my supernatural ears couldn't pick them up. The door was closed but I decided I wasn't going to let that stop me. I would act like I belonged, eventually I might feel like it.

I pulled it open and stepped in with a smile. "I brought you food, you have to eat as well as do your duty to the pack," I said brightly. Then froze at the picture in front of me.

Logan sat behind a huge desk looking like the perfect alpha surrounded by memorabilia of his pack and family. Perched on the corner of his desk looking annoyed by my interruption was a sultry Wolf I'd never met before. She had long blonde hair and bright green eyes. She wore a tank top that showed a lot of cleavage and low slung jeans allowing her flat belly to peek out. Her lips were perfectly pouty and I felt like a complete slob as I eyeballed her.

"How wonderful, you have a loyal staff here, I see, that will be important," the woman said, hopping off the desk and coming to take the plate from me. She swung her hips seductively and turned back to Logan. "Here you go, love, eat up while we discuss the future."

I was frozen until she said that, then anger fired up in me, and I stepped forward. Before I could slap some sense into the girl, Logan growled.

"Amber, you know very well that this is my chosen mate, Fawn, and I have no interest in discussing anything further with you. Out, before I call someone in to drag you out."

Satisfaction filled me, and I smiled as she shot me a harsh glare before stomping out with a huff. The door slammed behind her, and I was pretty sure I caught a laugh or two from the crowd. That must have been why so many were watching me approach the office.

"Amber?" I questioned with a raised eyebrow as I leaned down to kiss Logan.

He sighed and rubbed his face. "The daughter of the Northern California pack alpha. He thought he'd send her up here to try and make an alliance."

"And by alliance you mean marriage?" I guessed.

Guilt filled his features. "I should have warned you; I knew he was going to try it, but I thought he'd have the decency to wait a few months."

"Eat," I said, pushing the plate toward him. "You've been at this all day; you must be starving."

"Oh I am," he teased and grabbed me around the waist, pulling me onto his lap and playfully biting my neck. "I'm just not sure we won't be interrupted if I start eating what I'm craving."

I slapped at him and giggled. "You insatiable beast."

"Am I interrupting?" Lila said with a laugh. I hadn't even heard the door open.

"Yes," Logan growled at the same time I assured her no and pulled out of his arms.

"There was a small ice storm in the city and I got word that a few pack members are going to be pulling in right before the run. Wanted to give you a heads up." She looked at me. "We usually close the road down before the run to make sure we stay safe from unexpected visitors," she explained.

"Fuck, I should be there," I grumbled. Another storm, this wasn't good.

"No, you should be right here," Logan said, pulling me into his arms. "I need you too."

"And besides, who else is going to keep Amber's paws off of Logan," Lila pointed out. "She's currently snarling at everyone so I'm guessing you did good putting her in her place."

"I guess I did." Though it was really more Logan.

"Good, and I also came to tell you that Terrance is going to ask you about dating Jasmine."

"What," I gasped. Terrance was Logan's cousin and a nice guy, but Jasmine was in no position to date anyone.

"Yeah, he's mooning over her right now, I think the scent of her pregnancy is making him horny." She made a grossed out face.

"I think the full moon is making him horny," Logan grumbled.

"Damnit," I hissed and stalked from the room. Sure enough Jasmine was sitting on a couch and Terrance was close by her side talking quietly and smiling at her like she was something special.

"Terrance," I snapped.

All heads turned my way and my cheeks flared but I wasn't going to back down.

"Fawn," he said carefully, his eyes darting from me to behind me where I was pretty sure Logan stood in his office doorway watching.

"Come talk with me," I said before I could lose my nerve, then I turned and walked outside. If I was going to be Logan's mate, well then, I hoped that gave me a little authority with the pack. I could order a bit of respect.

Terrance did follow and I stopped in the yard away from the others where we'd have a bit of privacy to chat.

"What do you think you're doing?" I demanded.

He looked worried. "I didn't mean to offend you, Fawn."

"She's married and pregnant, Terrance."

"I know," he grinned. "I can smell it on her, but it doesn't bother me one bit."

Yuck. "You can't be messing with a married pregnant woman just because the full moon's got your panties in a wad."

He smiled at me and leaned close. "I think you're the perfect alpha's mate."

"Don't try to get on my good side," I snapped with a smile, but it did soften me to him. He'd always been nice to me.

"I know she's in the middle of a messy divorce. I know she's important to you. I promise not to hurt her. I can't help that she's my type."

How could I argue with that? "Good, I'd hate to tell Logan to eat you."

Terrance laughed and put an arm around my shoulder. "Since you're being so generous, I should warn you that Amber is after your man."

"Oh I know. But I'm not worried."

"You shouldn't be," he said. "That man is in deep with you and everyone knows Amber is a whore for any alpha, Logan isn't special to her, he's just a way to make daddy happy."

I almost felt sorry for the woman, almost.

As we walked back toward the house with way too many eyes on us, I felt good about my place in this pack. When we walked into the house and Logan growled at Terrance for having his arm on me, I felt even better. Terrance went back to sitting with Jasmine, who I gave a wink to and then kissed Logan firmly in front of everyone. When he walked back into his office followed by a couple of Werewolves I caught a death glare from Amber across the room, which I ignored as if she didn't matter even as much as the rabbit poop on my shoes.

I settled into the living room with Lila where I could keep an eye on Terrance and Jasmine. As long as she looked pleased and not pressured by the horny Wolf, I would let it happen.

"My mother used to handle most of the female issues that came up. I think if you defend them as fierce as you defended Jasmine there, you'll have a pack full of loyal women behind you."

"You know I would, pack or not. I can't help helping," I laughed.

"Lucky us," Lila said with a laugh.

"Excuse me, Miss Malero." A young Werewolf girl came up with head down and eyes averted, hands clenched together.

"Fawn's fine," I said quietly, unsure what this could be about, and she nodded nervously.

"Um, Miss Fawn," she whispered and shifted on her feet.

I looked at Lila who just shrugged. "It's Penny, right?" I knew I had met this girl before but wasn't sure I had her name right.

"Penelope," she corrected. "But you can call me Penny," she added hastily, nearly choking on emotion.

"Penelope, why don't you sit down," Lila said, vacating her seat for the girl who sat on the edge of the seat and stared at her knees until Lila walked away.

"I was hoping I could ask you for help, um, since you're our alpha's mate and all." She darted a look at Jasmine.

"Sure, even if I wasn't, you could still ask me for help," I assured her.

She flicked her gaze to me and quickly away. "I'm pregnant," she whispered.

Fuck. She looked twelve. "How old are you, Penelope?"

"Seventeen."

"And the father is?"

She bit her lip and shook her head.

"Okay, let's go somewhere else." I looked across the room and met Lila's gaze, giving her a meaningful head nod, then did the same to Jasmine. I hurried the girl from the room, up to Logan's bedroom, Lila and Jasmine following like bodyguards.

Penelope looked frightened as the door closed behind Jasmine.

"I promise they are trustworthy," I said indicating Jasmine and Lila. "When did you find out you're pregnant," I asked so that everyone in the room would know what was going on.

"Yesterday, I think it's too early for anyone else to notice." She flicked her gaze to Lila.

Lila nodded. "I can't smell it on you."

"Do you want to keep it?"

She nodded and sniffled.

"And you're afraid to tell your parents?" I guessed.

She nodded.

I looked at Lila for guidance, but she just shrugged.

"Does the father know?" I asked and she burst into tears, crumpling to the floor.

"He said he doesn't want anything to do with the baby or me anymore," she wailed.

"Asshole," Jasmine gasped indignantly. "Well, men are not necessary, I can attest to that," she added.

I was worried, this felt way above my abilities. "What exactly do you want me to help with?"

She looked at me and away quickly again. "My father is going to murder me when he finds out or force me to marry the father which I will *not* do. I refuse to be married to someone who doesn't love me." She hiccupped through her tears. "Unless the alpha supports me, I'm going to be banished or dead, and if I'm banished, I might as well be dead," she wailed.

Jasmine embraced her. "Oh sweety, don't worry. Logan is the nicest Werewolf I've ever met. He'll support you."

"Damn straight," I assured her. I looked at Lila and mouthed the word *banished?* Lila shook her head no. Must just be dramatic teenager ideas coming out.

"You won't shift," Lila pointed out, "Everyone is going to know you're pregnant tonight."

"That's why I had to talk to you now. I can't do this alone," Penelope pleaded.

"You aren't alone," I assured her. "I do think it's important that we know who the father is though. If he's a part of this pack, Logan needs to have a word with him about appropriate behavior."

"Jeremy Wittle," she whispered.

I didn't recognize the name, but Lila exploded with outrage. "That little dipshit!" She stormed out and I smiled after her.

"See, you've got all the support."

I helped Penelope dry her face and then took her to Logan's office to explain the situation. Lila dragged the offending male Werewolf in by the scruff of his neck. He was a scrawny kid the same age as Penelope it looked, and scared shitless. I think he was about to pee his pants when Lila threw him into the office and Logan looked at him.

"You have no desire to be mated to him," Logan asked Penelope.

"No," she whispered, shivering in my arms.

I glared at Logan; he was scaring her.

Logan took a breath and rolled his eyes. "We don't leave our packmates in trouble, Jeremy," Logan growled, and the kid cowered, making himself small.

The door burst open then and two sets of parents rushed in demanding to know why their kids were in the alpha's office.

Logan explained the situation while Penelope cried against my shoulder. Her parents looked shocked, but Jeremy's didn't and they glared at their son. They all started talking marriage and Penelope practically screamed as she cried about that. Logan demanded Penelope's dad accept his daughter's decision to be pregnant and unwed without punishment and demanded Jeremy's parents see to it that Jeremy took financial responsibility for the child starting now.

No one could argue with the alpha's decision, it was obvious the two weren't in love and way too young to be making the decision to be married, child or not.

When everyone shuffled out, I smiled at Logan. "You know I might be okay with this whole alpha's mate thing. I like helping people."

"I like you helping people. I don't think that poor girl would have come to me on her own."

"Definitely not, you're terrifying."

Logan pretended shock. "Am not."

"You make me shake in my panties," I said with a giggle.

Logan took a break then, locking his office door and proving just how much he could make me shake. When we walked out with equal looks of satisfaction on our faces it was almost sunset and time to get ready for dinner.

The pack feasted on full moon nights, and it was a formal affair. I dressed in black and wore the choker that Silvara had given me. Amber's eyes were drawn to it instantly, and she growled, then ignored both me and Logan the rest of the night.

When it was time for the pack to head out and run, I took Jasmine and Penelope upstairs to watch movies and eat popcorn. Neither of them lasted long and I ended up watching alone until Logan came in sweaty and naked to collect me from Jasmine's room.

I don't know why I even considered not coming. This was a part of my life now. Balanced with what the city needed me to be.

Chapter Eight

We arrived home late the next night. Logan had spent most of the day attending to any other needs within the pack and thankfully it hadn't included any more of Amber's bullshit. She'd taken off after the run, back to California I hoped.

"It's party night!" Zin said happily as she sauntered into my house after we'd just slumped onto the couch. She was in a short leather skirt and mesh top over a bright red bra. Drake swept in behind her like a bodyguard with love in his eyes. He smiled at me and inclined his head in greeting.

"Party night?" I asked.

"You look like a party girl," Logan said to his sister, not a compliment.

"Oh shut up, Logan. This is a special night, the wedding party arrived, and they want everyone out at the club."

"Is that why you weren't at Brakemoor?" I asked.

"Yeah, Drake had to be here to get things set up, lots of Vamps needing light tight rooms. Anthea and Kearne are popular."

"Kearne must be the happy groom?" I couldn't imagine liking the guy, but then again, he was the thing that had motivated Anthea to officially break her engagement to Logan so I owed him. I wouldn't mind meeting him, but I was not prepared to see Dante; had thought I wouldn't have to until the wedding and surely he would be far too distracted to try and seduce me at his daughter's wedding.

"You're coming, aren't you?" Zin said with a pout.

"Of course," Logan assured her, giving me a look that said we had no choice.

"Yay!" Jasmine called from the couch and Betina agreed.

"I'll call Annabel, she's always up for the club," I said, and the more people to distract Dante, the better.

"That's not very ladylike," Evie said shamefully.

"We aren't ladies," I assured her, and she grunted agreement.

An hour later we were standing outside the Vamp club being let in by a huge Vampire who had telepathic powers.

Lots of Vamprose Vampires tonight, and you show up with your Werewolf? He questioned me silently.

Not afraid of fangs when I'm with a guy who's got such big claws. I thought back and he laughed aloud in response making more than one of our group turn back and look. I didn't know how many were aware of his ability, but he seemed to like connecting with me every time I walked through the door, and it was a fun secret to have.

The club was packed as usual but despite the hundreds of bodies moving in the dim light, I had no trouble picking out Dante among them. He had a presence about him that demanded attention. His blue eyes looked up as we descended the stairway to the dance floor, and I quickly looked away. Logan gripped my hand so I wouldn't get lost, and I put my other hand on his arm reaffirming our relationship. I didn't have to look to know Dante was smirking at the show, he'd made his intentions clear, as well as his willingness to wait out whatever was happening between Logan and me. Vampires had time to kill.

Drinks were needed, so we went to the bar first. "Hey, Saul," I greeted the bartender who smiled at me brightly.

"Any luck on fixing our psychotic weather, Miss Malero?" He asked.

"Working on it. Any Vamps in here bragging about being the bad guy?" I asked with a laugh.

"You'd be the first I'd tell," he assured me with a wink and handed me a glass of wine.

"Brother!" Dante greeted Drake with a quick hug as he joined our group, then greeted the rest of us, hesitating on Jasmine. "This is a new pretty face."

Jasmine giggled and I rolled my eyes. "Jasmine, I'm a friend of Fawn's, new in town."

He gripped her hand lightly and laid a kiss to her knuckles. "A pleasure." He turned to me last, his eyes bright. "Fawn, it is immensely pleasurable to see you again."

Logan growled so low I only noticed because he was touching me, and I could feel him vibrate.

"Dante," I said, not offering my hand and it only made his eyes brighten and his lips quirk higher. He liked that he bothered me.

Logan pulled me to the dance floor and for a while we were lost to the music together. He held me closer than necessary, and I didn't mind at all.

"Are you trying to mark me up with your scent again?" I asked when he started kissing my neck.

He pulled away with a grin. "Maybe."

I just laughed and kissed him, hoping it was reassurance enough.

"Logan!" Anthea cried out, interrupting our dance and embracing him warmly. She pulled a tall, thin, and frankly sickly looking, Vampire behind her. "This is Kearne," she said excitedly introducing her fiancé.

"Nice to meet you," I said, offering my hand which he took in a surprisingly firm grip. I got the feeling he was far older than Anthea and had power wrapped up in that thin body that I didn't want to see let loose. I already knew he was politically powerful, physical power added to that made me nervous. My eyes were drawn up and I met the bouncer's gaze at the top of the stairs, he was watching our group carefully.

Who is he? I questioned the bouncer silently.

Son of the European lead Vampire. This marriage is going to change the Vampire world. He didn't sound happy about that.

I looked at Kearne with a new eye of caution. I supposed I would have known that already if I hadn't been avoiding anything to do with this wedding. Logan didn't look at all surprised by the man.

"Thank you for welcoming us to your city," Kearne said to me, and I couldn't help stepping away from his intensity.

"I'm sure my father is honored to have you two celebrating your wedding here," I said, not wanting to claim the city as my own, especially with the current issues. Something told me this guy wasn't a rabbit lover either.

He quirked an eyebrow but didn't comment on my deflection. "I expect the weather to be acceptable and the city clean of vermin soon," he said, undeterred.

I gritted my teeth. "I'm doing what I can."

Seemingly satisfied, he took Anthea's hand and pulled her away, she bounced happily beside him.

"Are all old Vamps stoic and entitled?" I commented as they were swallowed up by the crowd. Kearne's presence reminded me of Drake and Dante who were both quite old and a stark contrast to the writhing happy young bodies in the club. Though I wouldn't call Drake entitled, Dante did fit that description. I had to assume that at some point Vamps became that version of dark and dreary, probably after too many lifetimes of death and destruction weighing them down.

"Yes," Logan said and pulled my attention back to him and the music we were moving to.

I couldn't get back into it though, Kearne was going to hold me responsible if I couldn't figure out the issues in the city, and I didn't want on his bad side. I needed a plan, but all I had was a deadline.

We retreated to our drinks and Logan was pulled into a discussion with a few out-of-town Vamps about the recent troubles with Portland's Supes wanting to come out. I excused myself to find Jasmine.

She wasn't supposed to be left alone, but I'd spotted Tony showing up and knew that would take Betina away from guard duty and Annabel was never one to miss out on a good dance floor, so she was probably in the middle of it somewhere soaking in all the euphoria.

It was a good thing I went looking, because when I found her, she was backed into a corner by a blond haired, leather clad Magician.

"Maddox," I snapped, grabbing his shoulder and forcing him back a step only because I'd surprised him. I was under no delusion that I had any amount of strength over him.

"Back off, this is between her and me," Maddox yelled above the music.

"No, it's between you and me," I said, placing myself between Maddox and Jasmine.

"I can move you," he snarled and grabbed my shoulder. His grip was tight and there was a power pulsing off of him that made the air around me tremble.

"I suggest you remove that hand," Dante said with a dark calm that left no room for argument.

"This doesn't concern you, Vampire," Maddox said without looking away from me.

"That's where you're wrong." Dante grabbed Maddox by the hair and flung him back with an ease that both terrified and impressed me.

"Thanks," I said as I watched a crowd of Vampires surround the now scrambling Maddox. If he was lucky, they would just escort him out.

"Are you alright?" Dante reached out and gently touched my shoulder.

"Yeah. Jasmine, are you okay?" I turned to my friend who just looked pissed.

"What do I have to do to convince him it's over?"

"Get a lawyer," Dante suggested.

"What the hell happened?" Logan said, rushing forward.

"Maddox," I explained with a frown. "I think we need to hire Jasmine a bodyguard that won't be distracted by her boyfriend." Where the hell was Betina, she was going to get a talking to.

"I think I know just the wolf," Logan said with a wink and pulled out his phone and started texting. "Is everyone alright?"

"Yeah, I had it mostly handled, but Dante helped," I admitted.

Dante almost laughed. "Always a pleasure to throw around a guy with his hands on you, Fawn," Dante said.

You bring trouble, good thing Vamprose is on your side. Should I dispose of the offending Magician? The thought floated into my mind, and I didn't bother looking up to know where it was coming from.

I had a feeling he would more than just kick the guy out, and no one would find the body. I couldn't ask for that kind of violence. *No,* I thought back. *Just kick him out of the club with a warning to stay away.*

He won't be allowed in again. He assured me and I was glad I had a few good friends, as odd as they were.

I dragged Jasmine to the bathroom. "Are you sure you're alright?" I asked when the loud music was cut off by the closing door.

"Yeah, are you sure you're not in love with that hottie Vampire? Oh my god Fawn, he has got major eyes for you."

"Yeah, and a tendency to invade my dreams," I mumbled.

"What?"

"Oh Fawn," Anthea said coming in then, thankfully stopping Jasmine's questions. "Are you okay? My father said he had to save your life."

"Well, that's a bit dramatic. He just removed a guy whose hand was on me."

Anthea gave me a concerned look.

"Promise, I'm fine. This is Jasmine by the way, she'll be attending the wedding with Rex."

Anthea greeted Jasmine enthusiastically then left the bathroom again.

"Logan was engaged to her?" Jasmine asked.

"Yeah, they were young."

"She's probably the exact opposite of you."

"Maybe that's why he liked her," I said honestly. That was back when Logan hated me and blamed me for his brother being banished.

"But it didn't work out, so obviously he had a type, and she wasn't it."

I smiled because I liked being Logan's type and that meant Amber wasn't. She was blonde and bitchy. Anthea was dark and hyper. I was in between in both my looks and attitude.

"Ready to get back out there?"

"Honestly, I'm ready to go home. This baby has taken my party girl time down a few notches."

When we found everyone and exited the club, it was hailing and it felt like it had dropped about thirty degrees since we'd arrived.

"Damn," Betina complained, shivering. Tony embraced her and she sighed with relief.

"We can warm each other up," Jasmine said, pulling Annabel close.

Logan held me, sharing his body heat.

"We need to see the circle of impact. This is as good as the snow, it has to have a center," I said quickly. "What are the chances it's the Needle again?"

"I'll call the weatherman," Logan said.

A few minutes later Logan was off the phone with confirmation that it looked like it was centered around the Space Needle again.

"What if it's being used as an amplifier?" Logan said as he tucked his phone away. "We should go check it out."

"I'll take Betina and Jasmine home," Tony offered at Jasmine's obvious yawn.

"Thanks, Terrance will be here by morning to take on guard duty, so if you don't mind staying at least until we get back?" Logan asked and Tony nodded.

I hugged Jasmine and Betina; then Logan, Annabel and I hurried to the truck. I was hopeful. If nothing else, this proved we knew where the guy was likely to try again and if we had to stake out the place, that's what we would do.

Chapter Nine

It was the middle of the night, but what traffic there was, moved slow due to the weather. By the time we arrived at the Space Needle the hail had thankfully stopped and there wasn't a crowd this time so we were able to get right up to it and look for any clues left behind.

Logan stripped and shifted to wolf form so he could get a better sniff around while Annabel and I watched from a distance, not wanting to contaminate anything. We also weren't dressed for investigating, we'd be likely confused with prostitutes if we stood on the side of the road, so we stayed in the truck and waited to see if Logan could find anything. I pulled my pepper spray out of my purse, just in case, a girl could never be too careful.

"Kearne is creepy as fuck," Annabel said as we watched Logan skulk around, nose to the ground.

"He's some kind of bigshot in Europe I guess," I said with a shrug. "So she's marrying well I think, making some kind of alliance."

Annabel nodded, seeming impressed with my knowledge of Vamp politics. "You don't think it's a love match at all?"

I thought about that. "I don't know. I guess I'd have to see them together more to know for sure. It reminds me a bit of Drake and Zin. Total opposites on the outside but desperately in love with each other. Maybe Anthea and Kearne are desperate for each other too, I just haven't gotten to see it yet." I hoped they were, I was starting to like the girl despite her past with Logan and wanted to see her happy.

"Either way, they'll marry I suppose. Makes me glad Witches stay single. We might have a kid with someone to make sure it's born with strong magic, but we don't spend the rest of our long life with them for political gain."

"So you're not regretting sending Gildar away?" I asked.

"No. Elves marry for politics as much as anything. I don't blame my father for sending what he viewed as a good match my way, but I am not interested in Gildar," she said his name like it left a bad taste in her mouth.

"Do you think your father will keep trying to find you a mate?"

A smile lifted her lips, but she quickly straightened it out. "I don't know, perhaps he thinks it is his fatherly duty."

And perhaps she liked that he cared, I decided.

Having a child for strong magic, that had my mind spinning around Jasmine's situation. Was that why Maddox was so desperate to keep her with him? Because their child was likely to be powerfully gifted? Jasmine's ability to bring electricity to her fingertips mixed with his apparent ability to vibrate things around him in a smallish earthquake could make for a dangerous gift, of course that's not how Magicians got their powers, it wasn't inherited directly, it was random.

So no, he was just a controlling asshole looking to keep political face.

A streak of black flashed across the street in front of the truck. Someone was running, fast. I didn't think, I just reacted. I jumped out of the truck and chased. Whoever it was, I had some questions because no one ran that fast from a crime scene without reason. Thankfully, I'd worn boots with my skirt, so I pounded down the pavement without slipping or breaking an ankle, but I still lost the runner. He was too fast, and he'd had a head start.

"Damn," I gasped, hunched over and trying to catch my breath.

"What ya chasing?"

I screamed and reached for my pepper spray, but it was gone, I'd dropped it in the truck when I'd jumped out to chase the shadow. A woman stood there with a rabbit in her hands. Not human, I knew it immediately, but I couldn't place her right away which made me think Magician. She had red hair braided down her back and she was wearing jeans with a bright yellow jacket. She had on a backpack and hiking boots, looking very much like half the people who walked around Seattle. Her eyes were too black, giving her away as a Magician and she smiled at me as I quickly took her in and recognized her as one of my own. Not that I trusted her just because we were the same type of supernatural, I wasn't an idiot.

"Not sure," I admitted. "You aren't from around here," I said it like an accusation, and she didn't miss it.

"Rusty," she said, holding out her hand. I couldn't place her accent, it rolled in a way I didn't recognize, but I was guessing English wasn't her first language. "Just strolled into town a couple weeks ago. You must be Fawn Malero, I've heard you are in charge around here."

"My father is," I corrected and didn't take her hand, some Magicians could influence through touch, and I had no reason to trust her.

She laughed and dropped her hand. "True, but you have part of the city, and you fancy yourself a bit of a P.I., or so I hear, with quite a bit of success." She stroked the rabbit between its ears, one white and one gray, a black circle around its right eye. I could feel its contentment.

The animal's happiness was a good sign but I didn't like that she knew so much about me. I hadn't heard about any new Magicians in town, and that meant she wasn't following the protocol of introducing herself to the local leader.

Annabel caught up then, panting behind me with her shoes in hand, she'd worn heels, no good for running. "This isn't who we saw," she panted, looking at Rusty.

"I lost him, this is Rusty, she's new in town."

Rusty smiled at Annabel but didn't offer to shake her hand. Annabel eyed her speculatively.

"You'll need to go to my father if you plan to stay any longer," I told her and grabbed Annabel's arm to leave.

"Oh I will," she called after us and I had a feeling we were going to regret Rusty's presence in Seattle.

Logan was dressed and waiting by the truck when we got back.

"Someone ran from here, way too fast for me, so probably not human," I explained.

"I could smell it, definitely old magic and Warlock."

We had a suspect. That brightened my mood. We walked to the Needle so Annabel could take a look and feel.

"Woah, he's definitely using this thing to amplify. It's practically pulsing," she said, and I agreed.

"That's probably what set off the alarms the last time alerting the police." Even I could feel the magic flowing from the thing, it was sharp and deep, two things that meant powerful in my experience.

"If he knows we're onto him, he won't use the Needle again," Logan said.

"Maybe we'll get a reprieve then, at least until he finds something equally affective." I couldn't help but hope it would hold off until after Halloween and Anthea's wedding. Maybe I could concentrate on just one problem. As if the rabbits weren't still an enormously imposing problem on their own.

Just as I was thinking it, three rabbits hopped by completely unafraid of the predator standing there.

"What's wrong with those damn things?" Logan growled and I gasped. His eyes sharpened and snapped to me.

"I could feel it," I exclaimed. "She was holding a rabbit and for the first time I could sense the damn thing, these other ones, nothing, but that one was communicating like normal. She had a different rabbit, or a normal rabbit, or, I don't even know." In my excitement I babbled, and Logan looked at me like I had lost it.

"Explain," Logan demanded.

"There was a Magician down that way," I pointed down the street. "When I stopped chasing the Warlock, she was standing there, holding a rabbit."

"Do you know her?" Logan asked.

"No, but I'm going to find her." I started walking in the direction I'd just come. Logan and Annabel followed but we didn't make it far, shivering in the cold and no Magician in sight, we gave up and headed back to the truck after just two blocks. Rusty was at the top of my suspect list though; I'd find her again and her little rabbit too.

We got home as the sun was rising and I was exhausted. I fell into bed and curled up next to Logan, then drifted immediately off to sleep. My dreams were plagued by Dante's image and weddings that involved me as the bride and bunnies as the audience. No matter if I ran screaming back down the aisle, I still ended up in a room full of rose petals and one very sexy Vampire lurking in the corner. It was all very confusing.

Chapter Ten

My mood was sour when I woke up late, so finding Rex and Damien in my living room when I came down the stairs in search of coffee only made me want to turn and go back to the disturbing dreams. Jasmine greeted me cheerfully and Evie was tittering happily to have men in the house. Betina was hopefully already at the yoga studio.

"Morning," I grumbled.

"More like noon," Rex said accusingly.

I flipped him off over my shoulder as I went to the kitchen and poured a cup of coffee, thank goodness it was fresh. Jasmine must have made it when the guys showed up. I stared out the window and smiled at Terrance who was standing in the yard, taking his guard duty seriously. Chester tweeted good morning and landed on my shoulder. I patted the parakeet gently.

"Why are you here?" I asked my brothers from the kitchen.

"Dad had an interesting visitor this morning," Rex said.

"Rusty?" It would surprise me if she'd done as I'd told her, but it would also be a good sign.

"No, who's Rusty?" Damien asked and I just shook my head indicating Rex should continue.

"Dad's neighbor had some jewelry stolen," Rex explained.

The neighbors were human, and why should we care about their jewelry? I didn't say anything, just sipped my coffee and waited for him to explain.

"This is the third neighbor hit in the last week with small item theft, they wanted to alert Dad and work together to increase neighborhood security," Damien explained.

That did seem concerning, but anyone stupid enough to try and break into my father's house would be surprised by his lack of need for security, he was a powerful Magician and could knock someone on their ass with barely a thought. Though he rarely needed to show his strength in such a manner anymore.

"I'm not interested in neighborhood watch duty." I had enough going on.

"Dad's neighborhood isn't the only one being hit recently. Over the last two weeks dozens of people have reported jewelry and other small valuables missing with no forced entry and no evidence left behind," Damien explained.

I perked. "You think it's supernatural?"

Damien nodded and Rex just looked at me like he was gauging my ability to be in charge, he always looked at me like that, like he was waiting for me to fall apart so he could snatch my territory away from me and give it to Damien probably. I was in a bad enough mood I was tempted to throw something at him. He was lucky I desired my coffee more than breaking his nose open at the moment.

"Weird weather, rabbit plague, and break ins," I said thoughtfully. "What the hell is going on?"

"Dad wants all of us on this thing. With the wedding there's a lot of pressure on him to provide a safe city for the Vamps."

That I could believe, especially after meeting the happy groom.

My brothers stood to leave. Damien kissed Jasmine's cheek and Rex glared at him. "She's married, keep it in your pants Bro."

"Shit, I know," Damien snapped and glared at me as if it was my fault Rex was in such a bad mood. Maybe it was, but I didn't care if he yelled at Damien.

Jasmine's cheeks turned scarlet, and I pointed to the door.

"Let us know if you find anything," Rex snapped.

"Sure," I said noncommittally.

"Such nice young men," Evie sighed when the door closed. Jasmine and I both looked at her like she was nuts.

"Are you sure you want to be Rex's date to the wedding?"

Jasmine shrugged. "Like I said, might be my last chance to dress up for a while." She put a hand to her still flat belly.

"When did Terrance arrive?"

"Don't know, he was here on the couch when I woke up. He went outside when your brothers arrived and shot glares at him."

"If he makes you uncomfortable, I can have Logan send him away."

Jasmine blushed. "Oh no, he's fine."

Fine she said, and I smiled. She liked that flirty funny big wolf out there and that made me very happy.

Jasmine patted the couch seat next to her and I took it.

"He shut off my bankcard. I got a call today saying an order I placed didn't go through. He's waiting for me to get desperate and beg him to take me back." Fear filled her eyes. "I can't let that happen," she whispered. "My father won't help me, and now Maddox is taking away whatever he can."

I reached out and covered her hands where they sat protectively over her womb. "You can stay as long as you need, you know that. You have a job at the studio too, as long as you want it."

"Thank you but I can't stay forever, it's not big enough for all of us, add a baby to that and someone is going to crack, probably Logan," she laughed, and I was glad to see the tears were drying up.

"Yeah, Logan might not handle dirty diapers and crying babies in the living room too well. But we have a while before then and at that point we can just kick him out."

She hugged me and when she pulled away, I saw new tears in her eyes. "I told Betina I'd be at the studio by noon to take over the front desk, I better get ready since I'm already late. I needed the extra sleep today."

"I can text Betina and let her know you'll be in soon, go get ready."

She kissed my cheek and hurried away. She smelled like lavender, and it took me back to being sixteen for a moment.

Terrance came in, breaking me out of my memories and made himself a cup of coffee.

"You watch out for her," I ordered when he walked in.

"You know I will, Fawn." He took a long drink then gave me a serious look. "Can I be honest with you."

"I wouldn't want anything else, Terrance."

"I think you're good for the pack. I knew you would be good for Logan, you brought him up out of the darkness he'd been wallowing in, but I think you're really good for the pack too. Samuel would have demanded Penelope marry Jeremy and Logan knows that. I think he would have done the same thing, following his father's footsteps, if you hadn't been right there to intervene. You're going to bring an important fresh perspective to the pack."

"Which is why Amber was there; because tradition would have dictated that Logan marry her. It's a good political match and she's a Werewolf," I said, as if it didn't bother me at all.

Terrance nodded reluctantly.

"I get it, it makes sense. Traditions are hard to break. Too bad this big bad Magician is here stirring up trouble."

"As always," Terrance agreed and lifted his coffee in cheers.

I liked the idea of shaking up old ideals within the Werewolf pack.

"Ready," Jasmine trilled as she came out of her room dressed in yoga pants and a sports bra under a zippy jacket. Her hair was up in a high ponytail, and she looked like yoga barbie complete with hoop earrings and an ear-to-ear smile directed at Terrance.

"I'll drive you, my dear," Terrance said, setting his cup down and offering her his arm.

"Young love," Evie sighed when the door closed behind them.

"Jasmine's always in love with someone," I whispered, wondering if it was ever real for her or just fleeting and fiery. Should I worry that she'll lead Terrance on?

"Nothing wrong with being in love when you can," Evie said. "You never know when your chances will run out."

I couldn't argue with that. I'd gone a long time between loves, and it hadn't been full of happiness. Jasmine had broken my heart at sixteen and then I fell in love with Logan, just a bunch of mediocre relationships in between.

Evie didn't stick around for conversation, so I was thankfully left alone with my coffee and thoughts.

I pulled Pumpkin onto my lap and tried to think of a plan of action. Chester tweeted happily as he swooped in and perched on my shoulder, unafraid of Pumpkin. He wasn't a huge fan of Jasper and Sophia, but he'd realized that Pumpkin was far too lazy to try and catch him.

I stroked Pumpkin with one hand and lifted my fragrant coffee with the other. My thoughts drifted to the trouble in the city. There was a Warlock messing with the weather and Rusty had something to do with the rabbits, I was sure. Someone was stealing jewelry and other valuables using supernatural abilities, risking exposure, and there was a wedding on the horizon that couldn't be plagued by any of it. Well shit when it rained, it poured, in Seattle apparently.

The doorbell rang and I stared at it with a frown, which horseman of the apocalypse would this be? Hopefully not famine because I hadn't gotten breakfast yet.

I opened the door, my pepper spray stuck into the waistband of my sleeping shorts. A young Werewolf woman stood on my doorstep with red rimmed eyes from crying and hands clenched nervously. I recognized her from Brakemoor but couldn't recall her name.

"Logan's not here," I said quickly, assuming she needed something from her alpha.

She visibly relaxed and that made me tense up.

"I need to speak with you, actually, you're a private investigator. You have some kind of confidentiality with clients, right?"

Uh-oh. "I am," I said carefully.

She held out a wad of cash, pushing it into my chest and forcing me to take it. "I need you to catch my cheating husband and you can't tell anyone."

"Oh, um... I can certainly look into it, but I have a lot going on right now."

"Please, I need to know, I need to be the one to leave." She was desperate and upset and it prickled my supernatural empathy.

I ushered her inside and got her a cup of coffee. Once settled, she spilled her story. Her name was Patty, and her husband was Max. They'd married young, sweethearts right out of high school and they'd recently moved here to join Logan's pack. Her husband was working with Logan currently and she was in nursing school.

"Why do you think he's cheating?"

Tears streamed down her face at my question, and I regretted asking but I needed to know or I couldn't help her.

"I can't get pregnant," she sobbed. "He wants to be a father so badly, it's such a strong drive for all our men and I know that I shouldn't say anything, that it's expected for me to just let it happen, but I can't. I love him too much to share him with someone else." She wailed and the cats scattered.

I shook my head in confusion. "What do you mean expected?"

"Werewolf men; if their wife can't breed, then they go find someone who can. I should just accept it, maybe if I'm lucky whoever she is will let us raise the child." She hiccupped and sobbed some more. I scooted closer and hugged her until she stopped, then handed her the box of tissues.

"So you think that his cheating is acceptable by the pack? Just because you can't get pregnant?"

She nodded and I frowned. That was a new kind of bullshit I hadn't heard before.

"Maybe we should talk to Logan I'm sure—"

"No! No one can know, please, just find out for sure so I can be the one to leave. If I leave him, he is free to find someone else. If he chooses to breed someone else before I can leave, then I'll be ostracized for not doing my duty to the pack."

It was insane and I was ninety percent sure Logan would never ostracize someone for not wanting their husband to sleep with someone else. It was insane, but the laws in most supernatural communities were made so long ago many were very antiquated. None of that changed this woman's pain and her desire to know if her husband was cheating. No matter the reasons behind it, she deserved to know and make her own decisions accordingly. "Okay," I agreed because how could I not. But I was definitely going to be asking Logan about that barbaric practice.

When Patty left, I was feeling pissed off, so I called Annabel and told her what had happened.

"Is that how Werewolves treat their women?" she demanded.

"Honestly, I have no idea. Logan and I never talk about children in a serious way, or marriage. We're taking things slow."

"You need to find out before you get saddled with an asshole who thinks he can breed any female wolf that walks through the yard," Annabel snapped.

I loved Annabel and she was exactly right. She was also more than happy to try and catch a cheating asshole and when Betina got home, the three of us went on stakeout duty. If Max was cheating, we were going to catch him. I didn't tell Betina why he might be cheating, I didn't want her thinking badly of Logan and his pack if it wasn't true.

"How do we do this?" Annabel asked as we climbed into her car.

"Patty sent me a picture of Max and his truck. So I think we go to the jobsite and find the truck first, put a tracer spell on it and then we see where it leads. She said he's been telling her he works late, and she thinks that's when he sees the other woman. So if we're lucky, he'll head to her house right after work, in about an hour."

Unfortunately the guys had quit early, so when we arrived, the jobsite was empty except for Logan and we had to play it off like we were just in the area hoping to come across Rusty.

"I need a drink, why don't we head to Lila's bar and make a plan to trap a Magician and a Warlock?" Logan suggested.

It was as good a plan as any, so we parked outside Brews for Beasts a few minutes later.

We all froze when we walked into the bar. Sitting and chatting with Lila as she poured drinks was our man, Max, and the way Lila looked at him made me cringe. She had a bad history with picking the wrong men, worse than me even. If she was the one sleeping with our mark then I was going to have a really hard time telling Patty.

Without a word we strode to the bar and flanked the man, Annabel and Betina eyed him suspiciously and I looked curiously at Lila. "Hey, who's this?" I asked as if I hadn't met him at Brakemoor.

Lila looked surprised by my question and the other's hostility. "This is Max, he's new in the pack but you should have met him at Brakemoor, didn't you?"

"Max!" I said brightly and held out a hand. "That's right, I'm Fawn, Logan's girlfriend and local P.I. I think I met your wife too. Patty, isn't it?"

He paled slightly and took my hand in a quick shake. "Nice to meet you, Fawn. I was just heading out." He stood to leave, his beer not even half gone.

"So soon?" Annabel purred beside him and tapped his cup.

"Yeah," he whispered and nearly ran out the door.

"What the hell?" Lila snapped. "Why are you running my customers off like a bunch of nineteen twenties thugs?"

"He's a married man," Betina snapped back.

Lila put her hands on her hips and glared. "I know, they're in my pack."

"So what's he doing here?" I asked.

"What are you accusing me of?" Lila asked, her usual calm happiness gone, reminding me that she was a predator under her soft exterior.

"Nothing," I said simply. "Logan's on his way from work, we'll have beer."

Lila grunted and poured the beer. Logan walked in as she finished, and no doubt felt the tension but didn't ask. Just took the beer and immediately downed half of it.

"How was work?" Betina asked casually once we were all seated.

"Fine. Annabel, did anyone in your coven know anything about a new Warlock in town?" Logan asked.

She shook her head.

I told them about the burglaries and we all threw out ideas on who or what might be behind them. Logan called his packmate in the police department and it seemed that the spread of break ins and timing indicated a team of people not a single culprit.

"Shit, like a flock of fairies came to town and decided to steal shiny objects," Betina joked but I looked at her with wide eyes.

"What if that's it?" Fairies were rare but they existed, tiny little nuisances, they did like shiny objects and had no qualms about taking things that didn't belong to them.

"I hope not," Logan growled.

It was only human homes being targeted too, which made it even more apparent that it was a supernatural responsible. Knowingly avoiding homes where they would be likely detected.

"I think we should stake out my parents' neighborhood tonight, see if we can catch them in the act," I suggested.

"Sounds fun!" Annabel agreed quickly and Betina nodded. Logan agreed with less enthusiasm.

I had four problems to solve, and this suddenly felt like the most achievable.

Chapter Eleven

A couple hours later I was staked out on my parents' roof with a pair of binoculars enjoying the unseasonably warm weather in just a tank top and jeans. Logan was with me and Annabel and Betina were staked out along the fence closer to the street. They had a better view of the front of houses since my parents' house was tucked back a ways from the road for privacy, but we were high enough that we'd see the little bastards fly if it was fairies.

"Your turn." I handed the binoculars to Logan and laid back, staring up at the sky, it was super clear tonight. I could see a lot more stars than usual despite the city lights. "What don't I know about Werewolf society?" I asked, hoping I sounded casual.

Logan lowered the binoculars and looked at me curiously. "You're asking me what you don't know, how should I know what you don't know?"

I bit my lip and tried for a casual laugh. "Oh I don't know, just making conversation. It was interesting that Penelope was so scared about being pregnant and not wanting to be forced to marry, weird." It felt dumb but it seemed to satisfy him because he lifted the binoculars back up and hummed thoughtfully.

"I don't know, seems like it would have been pretty reasonable to expect them to get married. They liked each other enough to get pregnant, but I wouldn't have forced anyone to marry just because there was a baby involved," Logan said.

That made me hopeful, but I needed to dig deeper. "Tara's baby is getting big," I lied, I hadn't seen the half Werewolf half Witch in weeks, but he didn't know that.

"Oh yeah, it'll be interesting to see if he develops shifting abilities at puberty."

"Werewolves are pretty big on family," I said, unwilling to let the conversation die.

"Isn't everyone?" he said with a laugh.

"Yeah, but I think that Werewolves are more so. More than Witches and Warlocks for sure, gosh, Magicians usually have big families, but I've seen plenty not and you only have the two natural siblings whereas some of your pack has like seven, more like a whole litter and Trolls too they..." I paused because I had no idea. "Well yeah, Werewolves really care about kids." I finished weakly.

Logan cleared his throat, dropped the binoculars and stood up. "I think I'm going to run up and down the street and see if I spot anything." Then he jumped off the damn roof.

"What the hell!" I yelled after him, but he landed the three story drop and took off at a run toward the street as if the devil himself was chasing him.

My phone buzzed seconds later "Betina?" I answered.

"What's Logan after? He ran past without saying anything, did you spot something?"

"No, keep watching, he just thought he'd do some ground patrol." Or something I said spooked the shit out of him.

"Oh, cool. We haven't seen anything but a lot of rabbits, they're thick tonight, when do they sleep?"

"I don't know, I didn't think they were nocturnal animals, but maybe." I pulled the binoculars up and looked down at the lawns, there sure were a lot of rabbits, especially around one house in particular. "I wonder what they want with that blue house? Do they still have a good garden going?"

"I don't know, want me to take a closer look?"

"Sure, it looks like Logan's way down past it already." I couldn't even see him anymore.

Betina hung up and I watched as she hopped off the fence and crossed the street, then walked down half a block. The house that was attracting so many rabbits was a nice midsize blue house with two stories and a large front porch. It didn't look like there was much in the yard besides grass but maybe there was something about it that attracted them tonight.

"What are we watching?"

"Fuck," I hissed and would have slid off the roof if a very naked Anthea hadn't grabbed onto me with a laugh that was far too joyful for my almost accident.

"Sorry, I was out for a quick fly and saw you up here, figured it might mean something interesting is going on," she said cheerfully.

I wondered if Anthea's rare ability to turn into a bat increased her marriageability. Perhaps it was a trait that her fiancé was hoping to see in their children.

It was that ability that had gotten her into trouble a few months ago when she'd been trapped in bat form in a birdcage by a devious and obsessive human. I'd saved her before I'd found out she still thought she was engaged to my boyfriend. Not that I wouldn't have saved her if I'd known, I wasn't that jealous. She couldn't retain clothing with the shift of course, but she sat there as if it was no big deal to be naked on the roof in the middle of the night with me, so I just tried to ignore it, and really tried not to notice the heart shaped tattoo high on her right thigh and wonder if Logan had ever seen it.

"There have been some recent troubles with theft and we're staking out the neighborhood, it might be fairies because there's been no sign of breaking in or evidence left behind," I explained. "Pretty sure it's supernatural."

"Well I haven't seen any fairies around tonight, but that doesn't mean they aren't in the city, tricky little bugs."

I nodded agreement and went back to watching, though most of my attention was taken up with trying to figure out how far down Logan had run to get away from me.

Anthea looked perfectly content to stare out at the night in silence, but it was uncomfortable for me, I had to break it. "Where's Kearne tonight?"

"He doesn't shift," she said simply.

Okay... that certainly didn't answer my question. "Are you excited about the wedding?"

"Oh yes, Kearne is a great match for me. Father says that it will be the biggest match in history."

No mention of love. I gave her a sideways look. Her face was pure innocence, but I knew she wasn't young, in fact I was pretty certain she was older than Logan, Vampires just didn't mature quickly.

"Logan would have been fun, but we never would have been a quality match," she continued. "Werewolves are just so passionate!"

I bristled at her reminiscing her sex life with my boyfriend.

"Everything they do is big. Vampires are passionate too, don't get me wrong, I never would have agreed to a marriage without great sex. But he's so serious about the rest of his life." She sighed.

"I am sure you'll both be very happy." Because I didn't know what else to say and thanked the goddess when my phone rang so hopefully, I'd never hear Anthea talk about sex again. "Betina?"

"Nothing weird about the house or lawn, I don't know why it's so attractive to the rabbits."

I lifted the binoculars and saw her standing at the sidewalk in front of the house in question. "Okay, thanks for checking." I hung up the phone just as a movement caught my eye. The front door had a little flap where a cat could go in and out. It opened up and out slipped a rabbit. It was immediately embraced into the group and then as if it were one mind, the group started to leave the yard. "What the hell?"

"What is it?" Anthea asked excitedly, leaning forward, peering in the direction of the house.

"The rabbits are moving."

Anthea made a sound that indicated she was unimpressed with the development. "I can see that; they move all over this damn city. Really, I don't understand why the Werewolves haven't chased them out of town yet. The European Vamps are annoyed," she frowned. "My father says we have to make sure they don't call things off for me and Kearne."

"They aren't afraid of Werewolves. Hey, do you think you could fly along, see where they go? Maybe that will give us a clue as to what they're doing here."

"I can help with your investigation?" she said excitedly, making me feel bad for not being friendlier to the girl.

"Yeah, uh, if you aren't busy?"

"Awesome," she squealed then shifted to a small bat and off she went.

I called Betina and told her not to follow the rabbits, Anthea was on it. Then I looked around until I spotted Logan walking slowly back up the street. What the hell was his problem?

By the time Logan was stopped at the fence, obviously not about to rejoin me on the roof, I decided to give up the stakeout. The horde had dwindled to just a few rabbits hopping about and no sign of fairies or any other supernatural or human thief.

I climbed back in a window and found my mother and father sitting in the living room cuddled up and listening to music. They loved each other so much it was no wonder I had always expected my own epic love story to come along. I wanted what they had, I wanted to cuddle with my husband after a hundred years of loving each other with grown kids off doing their own thing.

"Any luck?" My mother asked when she saw me.

"Maybe, I sent Anthea after a horde of rabbits moving away from that blue house."

"The Peterson's?" My father said thoughtfully. "They haven't been hit yet."

"We didn't spot any fairies or anything else. Anthea hadn't seen any on her flight over either. So maybe we were wrong about them being the culprit." I shrugged, it was worth a shot, would have made sense. "Could be a group of Supe kids working together with enough know how to not leave evidence? If that's the case we should be able to catch them with a little work, hopefully return whatever was stolen too." I thought about the rabbit I'd seen come out of the cat door though and how one had poked its little head through the cat door in my own house. Luckily my cats had scared it off.

"Hey, do you know if the Peterson's have pets?"

"I don't know for sure, but I don't think I've ever seen anyone walking a dog in or out of there," my mother said.

"And what about the other houses that were hit, any of them have animals in the house?"

My father frowned and thought about it. "I know the Frank's house has been hit and they have two Great Danes."

"No commonality there. We are looking for a thief who isn't afraid of big dogs then."

"We will watch for all possibilities," My father agreed. "And the rabbits, why are they here?"

"I wish I knew," I huffed. "They won't talk to me, and they aren't afraid of predators. It's like they aren't all there instinctually." I shook my head, it didn't make sense, but it felt like the answer was right there, just beyond my fingertips.

"I'm sure you'll figure it out," my mother encouraged with a smile.

"What about the weather, where are we at with that?" My father asked.

I had hoped he wouldn't ask about that. I wanted to crumple under all the unanswered questions. "We spotted a runner from the Needle last night; we think he's using it as an amplifier for the spells and Logan smelled Warlock on it after the storm last night. That's all we have," I frowned. "Oh, have you heard from a Magician in town, Rusty? She has an accent. Red hair."

My father shook his head and my mother looked concerned. "What kind of accent?"

"I don't know, but I would guess English is not her first language."

"If she sticks around, I'm sure she'll be by, we all know the rules," my father pointed out.

The problem was, not everyone followed those rules as closely as he did. Most Magicians did, they were very black and white, right and wrong. Very little gray area for them, but every once in a while, a Magician was born without that natural instinct. Magicians like Stephan who was currently being held in a jail cell under my parents' house for selling magical items to humans. He'd gotten a stay of execution by telling me, very slowly, where and who he'd sold to so I could retrieve the items.

"We did get a visit from Maddox," my father said with concern. "You know he's quite determined to have his wife back and blames you for her staying away from him."

I put my hands on my hips and snorted. "She left him because he was abusive and controlling," I snapped.

"I know," my father said calmly. "She told me that when she first arrived. I informed Maddox that he has no rights in this city, I don't care who his father is. The problem is, Jasmine's father called me too. He's on his way to the city to try and mediate an agreement between the two."

Panic filled me. "I won't let him force her back into that marriage."

My father smiled and stood up, embracing me. "I would expect nothing else from you, Fawn. I can't tell him not to come, but I can offer a safe place for them to meet and be an observer to make sure everyone is playing fair. What happens from there is up to Jasmine."

What he didn't say was that I should stay out of it, and I appreciated that. I would support my friend as much as possible and I wasn't afraid to stand up to her father, especially with my own father in the room. Abuse was unacceptable, no one could argue otherwise. And a baby was no reason to be in an unhappy marriage.

"Thank you," I said.

"What are you wearing to the wedding?" My mother asked excitedly, changing the subject.

"I need to go shopping," I sighed. I wanted to look amazing, I wanted to be all Logan could look at.

"I'm sure you'll be beautiful. Just don't upstage the bride," she warned. As if I could, Anthea was gorgeous and no doubt her dress would cost more than my house.

I left the house and walked down to the fence where the others still sat watching the now almost empty street. Those rabbits were quick little critters, leaving behind a trail of poop.

Logan was there, looking stiff, his eyes darting around as if he were avoiding my gaze. "Anthea is following the rabbits?" Logan asked before I could comment on his weird behavior.

"She wanted to help," I shrugged. "I didn't give her my number though, so I'm not sure how she's going to let us know what she finds." Not to mention she was naked and obviously not carrying a cell with her.

"She has mine," Logan said quietly. "Hasn't changed in years," he added quickly.

"Of course, and Dante has mine," I said in a moment of jealousy that earned me a snicker from Annabel. "I assume she'll be returning to wherever he is staying after she's done flying around."

Logan stiffened slightly but gave no other indication that he cared Dante could have been contacting me in the last months.

Betina looked between the two of us, obviously sensing the undercurrent. "Maybe she'll stop by the house," Betina pointed out, which I wasn't sure I wanted to happen more than I wanted her to just call Logan with the information. A naked Anthea at the door sounded like a nightmare.

To be fair, Anthea had never done anything to earn my dislike and I couldn't hate everyone Logan had been with before me, that was just insanity. I actually think that

I would get along well with Anthea if I could stop thinking about her sleeping with Logan.

"There's been no sign of fairies or anything else. I say we give it up for tonight, see if the rabbits lead to anything," Logan suggested. "I didn't even smell anything out of the ordinary up and down the street. Which could mean that its local kids breaking into each other's houses as a prank and not Supes at all."

That would be an easy answer, which made me doubt it was going to be it.

The drive back to my house was uncomfortably quiet but I wasn't about to discuss whatever Logan's problem was in front of Betina and Annabel, so we all just sat in it. We swung by the Space Needle just in case, but it all seemed quiet. The weather was warmer than it should be, yes, but that could be explained away easy enough. No freak snowstorms, hurricanes, or hailstorms tonight, not even a particularly high wind.

"I bet we scared him, he probably won't do anything again for a while, or if we're lucky he moved out of town to torment another city," Logan pointed out.

I had a feeling we weren't that lucky.

Having nothing else to do but wait it seemed, we went home. Jasmine was already asleep, pregnancy made her exhausted and Annabel left with a stern look at Logan. She didn't know what the problem was, but she was obviously blaming him. I had to appreciate the unquestioned support.

Though I had no idea what his problem was exactly either. Something about our conversation had bothered him. I just wish he'd talk to me about it.

"All was quiet here, Boss," Terrance said, giving me a wink as we walked in. "I'm going to do a lap then I'll make myself comfortable in the basement." He gave Logan a serious look. "I'll come upstairs to watch all your girls when you head to work in the morning."

Logan nodded and Terrance walked out the front door.

"Do I count as one of your girls?" Betina teased.

"As long as you're under this roof with Fawn as your guardian," Logan said with a smile.

"Such a nice young man, I do hope he stays for a while," Evie said, staring out the kitchen window at Terrance.

"He's a Werewolf, Evie, I don't know if you're his type."

"Oh pish," Evie huffed. "Haven't you read Romeo and Juliet? Gang affiliation doesn't keep lovers apart."

Betina laughed loud and hard at Evie's wistful words and I rolled my eyes. "Gang affiliation, Evie. That's a stretch of an excuse, even for you."

She ignored me and continued to stare, happy with her compartmentalized reality.

"One of those rabbits came into the house today, straight through your cat door," she chastised. "I don't know why you keep those useless cats around if they don't eat the damn things that invade the house."

"I'm trying to figure out the rabbit problem," I grumped, the last thing I needed was Evie's opinion on the matter, but I was disappointed in the cats for not chasing it out this time. Why were they so determined to get in my house anyway?

"There's something very familiar about them, I just can't put my finger on it. I went outside earlier, and they flocked to me. I guess your animal attraction is rubbing off on me," Evie said.

That had me thinking. The things couldn't care less about predators like Terrance and Logan, they refused to talk to me, but they liked Evie? A ghost? Animals had a sense for the supernatural and often were the only ones in a human household that saw the ghosts around, but that didn't equate to attraction, more fear and unease usually. My own animals didn't accept Evie at first, it wasn't until I talked them through how safe she was that they treated her the same as the rest of us.

We settled onto the couch then to watch a movie with Betina. Terrance retired to the basement after ascertaining that the perimeter was clear. Pumpkin followed him down to steal body heat and cuddles I was guessing. Tony arrived to spend some time with Betina and I was just about to fall asleep against Logan's chest with Chester nestled in my hair when a knock sounded at the door.

"Anthea," I gritted out when Logan opened the door. I was glad she was going to let us know what she'd found when following the rabbits, unfortunately she'd flown over and when Logan opened the door with me safely tucked behind him, it was to a fully naked Anthea standing under my porch light.

"Oh my!" Evie screamed and popped out, apparently a bit of a prude when it came to female nudity. Logan turned around immediately, being a gentleman and Betina rushed forward with the blanket she'd been cuddling with Tony under.

"Cover that shit," Betina hissed. Tony stared, mouth open and shock all over his face. Poor kid was going to be in the doghouse with Betina for that.

"Oh, sorry," she said as she wrapped herself. "I wanted to come right away, no time to dress and drive," Anthea explained.

"Well come on in and have a seat then." I hoped the neighbors hadn't noticed.

We moved into the living room to hear what she'd seen on her rabbit following mission.

"I followed the rabbits and they joined with others too, a whole big mass of them moving through the city and then they ducked into a parking garage near the Space Needle. Under some hotel there and when I went in, they were all gone, just like they walked into a wall and disappeared into it! The craziest thing I've ever seen."

"No rabbits were left in the parking garage?"

"One, hopping around all alone."

I looked at Logan, but he seemed as confused as me. "I guess that proves the rabbits are a supernatural problem."

"Which makes them our problem," Logan agreed. "How many did you drop off at pet stores?"

I cringed. "Not a lot, forty, maybe more. Fuck, did I just slip supernatural rabbits into human homes?" I was going to have to make some phone calls tomorrow.

"Just because the problem is supernatural doesn't mean the rabbits themselves are," Betina pointed out.

That made me feel a bit better.

We thanked Anthea for her help and sent her on her way. I walked her out to the backyard so no one would see a naked woman turn into a bat and fly away. She assured us that she would be willing to help anytime and I felt like she was striving for a way to be useful. Logan said she'd never had a job in her life, and I guessed it was starting to weigh on her, being a socialite Vampire had to get old eventually.

Logan followed me up the stairs and I could tell something was bothering him. His steps hesitated and I thought he was going to make an excuse to leave, to go stay at his office apartment or something. I prepared to act unhurt. But he shut the bedroom door and undressed as usual. After I washed my face and slipped into shorts and a tank top, he was already under the covers staring at the ceiling deep in thought.

I cuddled up to him, my head on his shoulder and waited, hoping he'd tell me what was going on, but he just kissed my head and I soon fell asleep, worried.

Not surprisingly, my dreams were full of Dante. He held me close and whispered in my ear all the things he could do to take care of me. He stroked my hair and kissed my neck. I felt my body start to give in to his promises and passion. It would be so easy, he would take care of everything, control everything... is that what I wanted, to completely give myself over to another's control?

No, I had worked hard to become something I was proud of, I didn't want to give that up.

Give me a relationship with a little fight, an argument here and there, let me win sometimes and I'll let you win some. That was what Logan and I had.

I met Dante's eyes and he let out a frustrated sigh. "Not yet?" he said darkly.

"Never," I whispered and wished it was firmer. His smile told me he had heard the uncertainty there.

He pulled me tight and kissed me deeply, I forgot for a moment to fight against it, but a memory of Logan rose in my mind, and I pushed against the Vampire trying to steal my soul.

I woke with a jerk before the sun. I pressed myself against Logan and breathed in his comforting scent.

"Bad dream?" Logan grumbled and pulled me on top of him.

"Yeah," I mumbled against his bare chest knowing that no matter what was bothering him tonight, it wasn't something that would keep us apart and there was nothing Dante could offer me that was better than this man. Logan was everything I wanted.

Chapter Twelve

I woke up to Logan's frisky touches and by the time he left for work and I stumbled down for coffee, I was reaffirmed in our relationship status. He owed me some answers, but he wasn't the only Werewolf who did, so I called Lila and guilted her into meeting me for lunch. Luckily, I didn't have to face Jasmine yet, she'd gone to the yoga studio early with Terrance tagging along. I wasn't looking forward to telling her that her father was on his way to town and demanding a meeting with her and Maddox.

I called Annabel to help with the investigations, and we decided to check out the parking garage Anthea had followed the rabbits to before lunch. I'd called the pet shops that morning to see if they still had the rabbits I'd dropped off. I was relieved, and a bit disturbed, to hear that they'd all disappeared the night after I'd left them, which probably explained why they hadn't agreed to take more. At least I didn't have to feel guilty about supernaturally influenced rabbits being kept as pets.

"Do you know if anything was taken from that house we were watching last night?" Annabel asked.

I hadn't heard, but there was no reason to assume the neighbors would tell my parents if it had. Humans didn't know my father was any kind of authority figure. I texted my dad anyways in the hopes they had heard something through the neighborhood watch, then walked down into the parking garage with Annabel. It looked like any other parking garage, a bit small, but Seattle was cramped for space.

I stood back and watched as Annabel walked the edges, touched the walls, and came back with a confused look. "Are you sure this is the place?"

"I think so, I guess maybe I'll ask Anthea to show us tonight, to be sure. You didn't sense anything?" It was frustrating to think we could be looking in the wrong parking garage. How could a huge horde of rabbits walk in and disappear without leaving any trace of magic behind?

"Nothing, which means it's either the wrong place, or the guy is covering his tracks really well."

"Damn." Dead end, at least for now. We walked over to the Space Needle and the magic residue on it was still palpable. Annabel wanted to get a better look and decided to ride up to the top, but I decided to stay down, and watch the rabbits hopping nearby, if they started to head into that parking garage I was going to follow.

It was a warm day and even in my tank top and jeans I was feeling overdressed. But I'd had to wear boots, I didn't want to risk rabbit poop in sandals again.

I was watching the elevator go up and up when a prickling on the back of my neck had me turning just in time to see a red braid, yellow jacket, and green backpack hurrying down the street.

Rusty.

I ran for her, that woman was just too suspicious to ignore. The timing of her arrival and the fact that she didn't introduce herself to my father. It added up to no good.

I kept one hand on my pepper spray as I pushed past a crowd of tourists and gained quite a few choice words and hand gestures from the locals mixed in, but I didn't stop. When I was close enough, I reached out and grabbed the woman's shoulder, forcing her to stop so suddenly I plowed into the back of her, and we both fell forward into the street.

A car braked to avoid running us over, tires squealing as it darted around us and swiped into another car before coming to a stop. I had just caused an accident, fender bender really, but I didn't care, Rusty was going to give me some answers about why she was in town.

We'd rolled a bit and I forced her down so that in the end I was straddling her, and she was face down on the pavement. I had a big smile of satisfaction on my face. Until I got up and she stood, brushing rabbit poop off her jeans, looking furious with a suspicious brown smear on her cheek. My heart sank. Her face was covered in freckles, her eyes were bright green, and she was definitely not Rusty.

"Oh, sorry," I said weakly.

"Are you fucking insane?" She snapped. The gathered crowd was offering to call the police and giving me looks that resembled an angry mob out for blood.

"I tripped on one of these damn rabbits," I said belligerently. It wasn't a bad excuse really.

The drivers from the vehicles that had crashed were arguing loudly now and the driver who'd swerved out of our way was gesturing at me. This was bad. I didn't really want to deal with the police, so I did what anyone in my position would do. I threw an apology over my shoulder as I ran, fast, and I didn't stop until I was certain no one had followed.

I really hoped no one had recognized me from my yoga studio, this could be really bad for my human business.

When I was gasping and leaning against a building in an alley, I pulled out my phone and texted Annabel so she'd know where to pick me up. No way was I showing my face back there again until the witnesses were gone.

As I waited and caught my breath, I watched a few rabbits hop around. I crouched and tried to beckon them closer.

"Come here you little monster," I whispered sweetly. I waited and one got close. I tried to pour all my power into feeling the damn thing but came up empty. No thoughts, no feelings, nothing. It was like staring into a blank space. "What *are* you," I grumbled as it hopped away.

Annabel showed up shortly after looking like she was barely holding back laughter. "Did you tackle someone and cause a car accident?" she asked when I hopped into the passenger seat.

"I thought it was Rusty. I wasn't going to just let her walk away from me without answers this time."

Annabel nodded. "I thought I saw her too when I was at the top looking down at the two cars and people yelling. Yellow coat, red hair, and backpack? Right?"

"Exactly, but it wasn't her, this girl had freckles and green eyes."

"Accent?"

"Not that I heard when she was accusing me of being a psycho," I laughed.

"Dang, so you *did* cause the accident," she laughed.

"Unfortunately." I had also ruined my jeans, ripped holes in the knees and a layer of skin too, they were bleeding slightly and stinging now that the adrenaline was down. Somehow, I'd managed to dodge most of the poop, though not all of it. "Someone really needs to be out there poop scooping the city."

"I think they are, it's just too much to keep up on. So you tackled her and realized it wasn't the right girl, then you just ran away?" Annabel laughed.

"What was I supposed to do? Let the police arrest me for assault and causing an accident?"

Annabel shrugged, "No, I guess you really didn't have a choice. At least no one got pepper sprayed or stunned to passing out this time."

I was learning, I don't pull weapons first anymore, at least not in public.

When we arrived at the diner to meet Lila, I cleaned up my knees in the bathroom as best I could. When I came out Lila was sitting with Annabel.

She gave me a careful look as I sat down. "You tackled an innocent human and caused a car accident?" Lila asked after the waitress left with our orders.

I glared at Annabel. "Traitor."

"What else were we going to talk about," Annabel said innocently.

"I thought I saw a suspect."

Lila took a drink of her water, but I could tell she was trying not to laugh, and I was glad Annabel had told her, it lightened the mood at least.

"Lila what kind of views does the pack have on pregnancy and fertility?"

"Oh my god," she squealed and spit her water. "You're pregnant!"

"No," I hissed quietly. "God no." She looked at my stomach and I covered it protectively. "I am not pregnant damnit. I am too young and too not married to Logan for that right now."

She rolled her eyes. "So then do you plan on getting pregnant soon?"

"No, damnit Lila. Just answer me."

"Is this about Penelope still? Because I think that got handled as good as it could have," Lila insisted.

"No, not exactly," I wavered, unsure if I wanted to just come out with my question. I didn't want to violate Patty's trust.

"Werewolves love babies. If you got pregnant unexpectedly, Logan would be ecstatic, so would Mom and me, and Zin. Oh, it would be the cutest damn thing, oh Fawn I'm so happy for you."

"Lila, not pregnant, not getting pregnant." I was just going to have to come out with it before she continued to spiral. "If a Werewolf wife is infertile does the husband have the duty and drive," I hesitated, "And blessing, to just go knock up any hoe in the pack?"

"No! God, what do you think of us. I know shit like that used to go down, but our pack has been over that for a long time. Same reason we don't give females to the strongest in the pack anymore. Its antiquated bullshit that was meant to keep the females lower than the males. My father changed all that as soon as he came into alpha. Why?" Her face paled. "Oh no, are you not able to..."

"I'm fine," I said quickly. "I'm sure I'm fine, everything works just fine. This is professional interest." I gave her a meaningful look hoping she'd connect the dots. They did after a second.

"Max?"

I nodded. "I can't say for sure but, a woman came to me upset that her husband was going to go get some other Werewolf pregnant because she found out that she's infertile."

Lila's cheeks reddened. "He was a little flirty with me, but I didn't think much of it. Damn, he was trying to knock me up so he could give his wife a baby? I just figured they were on the outs, and he was hoping to get lucky. I wasn't going to, I don't mess with married men, I make bad enough choices without adding that to the mix. I was just hoping for a good tip." She shook her head. "That poor woman."

The relief I felt was enormous and my shoulders slumped. I had really not wanted to think that Logan would be okay with that sort of thing, or that Lila would be messing around with a married man. "Yeah, okay, I just needed to be sure that it wasn't something Logan permitted before I move forward with this little investigation. I'll follow the guy a bit and see if he meets up with anyone and let the wife know. Maybe I can get her to talk to Logan herself, or at least let me talk to him for her. He might need to reiterate how things are run in his pack if she thinks it's still the way of things around here. I hate to think what kind of pack they left behind."

"Yeah, they obviously don't know we aren't so traditional. Though they should. Our alpha's mated to a damn Magician after all, and his sister is a Vampire. I'd think the nontraditional thing would be what attracts a lot of younger Wolves out here away from those high mountain packs like they have up in North Idaho, that's a very traditional group."

"I'll trail him today when he leaves the jobsite and see if he meets up with someone. Hopefully he doesn't head to your bar," I said with a pointed look.

"If he does, I'll be curt, and I'll ask after his wife as I make sure he knows I'm Logan's sister. New wolves don't always make that connection immediately. He certainly knew who *you* were though," she pointed out. "Logan talks about you, well, more like warns anyone he comes across to stay away from his woman," she laughed.

I liked how that made me feel. His protectiveness was comforting, especially since it came with a lot of trust and acceptance now. It used to feel overwhelming and a bit suffocating, but I was getting used to it.

The mood lightened as we talked through our meal then we hugged our goodbyes and I headed to the yoga studio for a bit. I needed to catch up on some paperwork and teach a couple classes since we were still short a girl. Jasmine and Terrance were already gone by the time I got there and Betina was behind the counter with Sam, my daytime manager.

"That hottie with Jasmine, is he taken?" Sam asked with a seductive lick of her lips. "He reminds me of every naughty dream I've ever had," she added with a wink.

Betina giggled and practically ran from the room. It wasn't unusual for a supernatural to dally with a human, but it never worked out. Even if I did think Terrance would be interested in Sam, which I only didn't because he seemed to be so interested in Jasmine, I wouldn't encourage their relationship. It would end badly, with Sam hurt.

"He isn't taken necessarily, but he is chasing Jasmine," I said casually.

She frowned. "That's what I thought, he watched her like she was a damn sirloin steak. I was just hoping it was part of his bodyguard duty," she sighed dramatically. "Does he have a brother?" she asked hopefully.

"What's got you so desperate today?" I teased, hoping to change the subject. Terrance didn't have a brother, but he had a hundred packmates that would readily agree to take a cute girl like her on a couple of dates.

"It's just been a while, you know."

I did know, I'd had a few dry spells in my life. "You'll find someone when you're not looking," I assured her.

"When Logan stumbled into my house I was definitely caught off guard." Partly because he'd been dragging a half-dead Vampire.

"I suppose, I'll wait for Prince Charming, or Mr. Right Now," she laughed.

By the time I was done with the classes I needed to teach, I was in a rush to follow Max. But I needed to not be seen by Logan or any other pack member who knew my car. So I decided to borrow Sam's with the excuse that I wanted to surprise Logan and needed to go incognito. Unfortunately, she drove a boat that had been her grandfather's and held sentimental value apparently. It didn't lend itself well to blending in, or parking. I had to park almost too far away to actually see Max's truck, but at least no one was going to be able to guess what I was doing here. I sat in the car and waited, Logan usually quit about four and it was three forty-five. So I shouldn't have long.

The weather was hot again, almost hotter than yesterday and I tried to roll down the window, by hand crank, and let in some fresh air but it was stuck. The car smelled like old cigarettes and aftershave. I was guessing Sam liked the smell because it triggered memories of her grandfather, it just made me a little nauseous, especially with the heat.

Pretty soon my stomach was churning, and I regretted not taking a shower to cool off before I left the studio. I was already heated from the workout and the smell was going straight to my head. After about ten minutes, I knew I wasn't going to make it.

I shoved the driver's door open and jumped out just in time to puke up everything that I had eaten at lunch.

Which is where Logan found me, leaning against the car with my eyes closed and gulping in breaths next to a pile of puke.

"Shit, Fawn," he whispered and pulled me into his arms. He stroked my hair and kissed the top of my head.

"I'm fine," I mumbled against his chest, but didn't push him away. My cover was blown, Max was probably already gone, and I liked when Logan hugged me tight.

"Why are you here in Sam's car?"

Of course he'd know the car, he paid attention to everything. It had been a stupid choice for many reasons.

"Oh, my car was acting funny, so I borrowed Sam's. I wanted to surprise you after work, but this is not what I planned," I said with a nervous laugh.

He gave me a look that assured me he knew I was hiding something. "I'll follow you back and take you home," he said gently. "We're done here for the day."

I looked up the road and saw that Logan's was the only truck parked in front of the site now, damn, I was really not hitting this P.I. thing well. "I don't need you to take me home."

"Fawn, I am not letting you drive your car if something is wrong with it. I'll have Tony check it out in the lot and if something needs done that he can't handle, I'll get it to a shop."

"Oh, yeah, thanks." Because how could I argue without telling him I'd lied?

As much as I didn't want to, I got back in Sam's car and made the hot smelly drive back to the studio. When I jumped out of the car, I nearly puked again but managed to hold it back, just barely. I took Sam's keys inside and left them under the counter, she was teaching a class and I was glad I didn't have to face her and tell her what her car had done to me.

When I hopped in Logan's truck his hands were gripping the wheel tight, and his jaw was clenched. He pulled out into traffic before talking. "Fawn, you know I love you and I want to make a life with you," he said without looking at me.

I reached for the door as his words hit me, but I didn't want to kill myself in traffic to avoid him breaking up with me or whatever this conversation might be leading to. After the way he jumped off the roof last night, I didn't have a good feeling about things.

"Yeah, of course," I said, desperately trying to think of something to say to distract him. "I caused a car accident today."

He nearly hit the car in front of him as he jerked his attention to me and back to the road. "What the hell Fawn! You have to be more careful!"

"I didn't say I was *in* an accident, Logan. I said I *caused* an accident. I thought I saw Rusty, chased her down near the Space Needle and we sort of fell into the road. It was really just a fender bender." I rubbed my knees; they were still tender.

Logan let out a breath as he tried to calm himself, maybe I should have picked something else as a distraction. "Maybe you should take some time off from the whole P.I. thing? Let Rex and Damien figure out the city's trouble?"

"Why?" I snapped. "I thought you supported me. I thought you believed I could do this." I crossed my arms over my chest and glared at him, but he refused to look at me. It hurt to think he didn't trust me, didn't support me.

"I won't have you endangering yourself, not—not now."

"Why not?" I demanded.

"Damnit Fawn, I know you're pregnant and I'm sorry I didn't react the way I should have last night when you tried to tell me but you can't go around putting yourself and our child in danger!"

Speechless, I was speechless, and I just stared at him with my jaw hanging open.

"I'm happy," he said gruffly. "It's unexpected, but I wanted kids someday, with you, and now is fine."

"Fine, now is fine?" I snapped, suddenly angry that he wasn't more happy about our nonexistent child.

Logan tensed, still refusing to look at me as he weaved through traffic. "There's a lot going on now, big changes already, and I thought we'd have more time before this happened. I thought we'd get married first at least. Fuck," he ran a hand through his hair and glanced at me. "We should get married."

"No."

"No?" he exploded and nearly sideswiped a car as he jerked the wheel and glared at me. "What do you mean no? You're pregnant, I love you and we *will* get married."

I rolled my eyes and debated letting him go on thinking I was pregnant and not wanting to marry him as punishment for only wanting to marry me because I was pregnant. But I relented. "I'm not pregnant, you asshole."

I swear I saw a flicker of disappointment cross his face before he turned back to the road and his body relaxed. "You're not pregnant?"

"No."

"Then what was with that conversation last night and the puke today?"

"Morbid curiosity," I said with a sigh. "And Sam's car stinks."

We didn't talk the rest of the drive and when we got home, I went straight to the shower. I needed a minute.

Chapter Thirteen

Tony dropped off my car, everything was working fine he said with a confused look on his face. I just smiled and acted like I had no idea the noises it made were normal. Sometimes being a girl has its advantages.

Lila texted to tell me that Max had not shown up at the bar tonight and Patty texted to say he'd come home right after work. I assured her that Logan didn't encourage cheating and asked her to speak with Max and Logan about the situation. She refused again and pleaded with me to keep watching him. I told her I would, but if I didn't find anything by the next full moon, then she needed to talk to Logan or I would out her in front of him at Brakemoor.

Jasmine was cooking dinner when I came down dressed for an evening of P.I. work; black jeans and black T-shirt, leather jacket in hand just in case a storm started up, and boots, in case of weather or rabbit poop. Terrance and Logan were outside trying to shoo most of the rabbits out of the yard and Betina had disappeared with Tony on a romantic walk in the warm evening. I had no excuse not to talk to Jasmine about her father.

"Hey Jasmine, how are you feeling today?"

"Great, I got a nap this afternoon, that helped. It was easy to drift off knowing Terrance was nearby watching out." Her gaze drifted out the kitchen window to the Werewolf in question.

"He's a great guy, Sam thinks he's a super hottie."

Jasmine stiffened and mashed the potatoes with extra vigor. "Oh, well, I am sure he'd love to know that."

I rolled my eyes. "Oh stop, you know he likes you."

"Yeah, but I'm pregnant and married, I don't expect him to actually want to date me and I'm not interested in a one-night stand, as amazing as I'm sure it would be. Which I already told him at Brakemoor."

I knew Terrance wasn't deterred by her being pregnant, or married, but I had warned him to take it easy with her so maybe it was my fault Jasmine was unsure. I'd have to talk to him. "I think he's being respectful of your status, that's all."

She grunted over the potatoes.

"My status is currently horny on pregnancy hormones," she muttered.

I chose to ignore that and push forward with what I needed to say. "My father has been contacted by Maddox *and* your father," I said, knowing it was best to just get it all out there."

Jasmine gasped and spun to stare at me, mouth gaping and eyes filling with fear. "I have to leave."

"No," I said quickly, grabbing her shoulders and making her focus on me before she spiraled. "No, my father is not going to force you to stay married, but he can't deny your father's right to come talk to you. He's going to mediate a meeting between you all, and I'll be there to support you. Don't worry, no one is being forced to stay married on my watch."

She pulled her arms around her stomach protectively. "And the baby?"

"Maddox will have rights to the child of course, he's the father. Unless he proves to be a danger to the child, do you think he'll be violent with the child?" That would change everything.

"Honestly, I don't know. He doesn't even like kids. He only wants what this one might be, powerful, rich, connected." She shook her head and her face twisted in anger. "I never should have let this happen.

"He can't take it from you. No one can. Even if he demands some rights, it can all be negotiated."

"I don't want him anywhere near me or it." Tears sprang from Jasmine's eyes just as Terrance walked in.

He rushed across the space and pulled her against him, glaring at me. "What the hell, Fawn?" He snarled.

"Watch it, Terrance," Logan growled a warning.

"Boys!" Evie snapped. "No one needs that kind of masculinity flying around right now."

For once, Evie was spot on.

Jasmine pulled back and looked at Terrance. "I am going to have to talk to my father, he's coming to Seattle," she explained. "I'm going to have to face Maddox and he is going to want this baby, *my* baby."

Terrance pushed her head back against his chest in a fiercely protective move that made my heart stutter for them. "I'll be by your side, you're facing none of this alone, Jasmine." Terrance looked across the kitchen meeting Logan's eyes and I could tell he was looking for approval from his alpha. This felt like way more than a fling he was wanting. He had more than a mild passing attraction to her. He wanted Jasmine as his own and he was willing to take on the baby as well.

Logan looked at me and I nodded, I had no qualms about Jasmine being in a relationship with Terrance. Logan looked at Terrance and nodded.

He swept her into his arms, she protested weakly as he strode from the room, carrying her like a child back to the bedroom.

"Oh my," Evie said, fanning herself.

"I guess I'm finishing dinner," I said with a frown. Jasmine had been cooking chicken it looked like. Gross.

Logan laughed. "I've got it."

"My hero," I mocked, and kissed him before fleeing the offending kitchen.

We had a plan to stake out two places tonight, luckily, they were both close to each other, so we rented a room at the hotel with a view of the Space Needle and the questionable garage underneath. If the Warlock showed up to amplify his magic again, we'd be ready, and if rabbits entered the garage in droves, we'd also be ready. I was eyeballing the street for a redhead in a yellow jacket too, sure Rusty was somehow involved in something.

The news was on in the background and talking about the heatwave, the weird storms, the rabbits, and the recent uptick in burglaries. All reminding me that I was failing. Neither Logan nor I wanted to talk about the pregnancy misunderstanding and marriage demand, which left a tension between us palpable enough that Betina, Tony, and Annabel had chosen to stake things out from the ground rather than watch with us in the room.

It was almost midnight when Logan spotted a shadow moving near the Needle. About ten minutes later rain started to fall, not just a little rain either, it was a torrential downpour and the wind picked up with it, fast and hard, hammering the rain against the windows.

"Damnit, he's at it again," I hissed, and we rushed out of the room. "At least this will take care of most of the rabbit poop."

"Thank god," Logan said, and I had to imagine his Werewolf sense of smell was particularly irritated by the scent with the heat amplifying it.

I followed Logan as we went, and I had my pepper spray and stun gun tucked into my belt in case I needed them. The little prick was not going to get away tonight.

We took the stairs and rushed out to the street. I was nearly knocked on my ass with the force of the wind, but Logan grabbed my arm and we rushed to cross the street. Betina and Annabel were already there wrestling with a shadow.

"I'm trying to fix it; I have to fix it!" The words floated to us on the wind followed by grunts as fists flew.

Then the Space Needle was struck by lightning and all four bodies were thrown across the grass with a terrifying sizzle.

The smell of hot metal filled the air, and thunder so loud I was momentarily rendered deaf, echoed off the buildings. Logan dropped my arm as we raced to our friends. Betina was closest and when I sunk down by her side, I gagged at the smell of burnt flesh and rotten fish that was coming from her. Logan pressed a hand to her neck feeling for a pulse.

"Alive," he yelled and rushed off to check Annabel and Tony. I touched Betina's face and prayed to whatever goddess might be listening that she'd be alright. Who did Trolls worship? I pressed my hands to her face and sent my healing senses into her. I latched onto the small spark flickering out and poured myself into it. I opened myself to the ability I was only beginning to trust I had. I welcomed its power and believed in it because the alternative was far too horrible. I felt it strengthen. I would not let her die; I would not lose someone I loved so much. I shivered as the feeling of completely giving myself over to the ability ran through me and into her. The little flicker became a flame and her head lit up with new flames as life renewed inside of her, strong and sure. It gained a footing with my help, then took on its own ability to heal her.

She was strong but damn, that had been the biggest lightning bolt I'd ever seen. The rain stopped and the wind died, as suddenly as the storm had come, it was gone. The sky cleared and as I looked around, I saw Annabel sitting up with Logan's help and Tony stumbling my way. No one else.

"Fuck," I hissed. We'd lost him and why the hell wasn't Betina conscious? I turned back to her and checked her pulse as Tony fell beside us.

"Is she okay?" he gasped in fear.

Her pulse was steady, but her eyes were closed. "I think so," I assured him and leaned close to her ear. "I'm going to be so mad at you if you don't wake up, Betina," I whispered and swallowed the lump forming in my throat. I loved this girl, and I was responsible for her being here. I pressed my hands to her chest, feeling her heartbeat. I could see her chest rise with her breath; she was alive I assured myself again. I laid my hands back on her head and was further reassured that it was still lighting up with life, whatever I'd done, it was working. I could sense my magic inside of her, working to support her natural healing.

I closed my eyes and steadied my breath, keeping contact with her as spectators started to stop and stare. I felt Logan and Annabel approach then heard them reassuring spectators that all was well and encouraging them to move along. No need to call an ambulance. I opened my eyes and sighed. "I think she's okay, but we should get her dry and home to bed." She was healing, but I had a feeling it would be a few days before she'd be really okay.

Tony pulled her into his arms and stood as if she weighed nothing.

I turned to Annabel. "What happened?"

"I'll get the truck," Logan said, rushing off. Annabel sat beside me looking dazed but otherwise okay. I put a hand on her, searching for damage done. She'd gotten a good shock, but otherwise seemed alright.

"We saw him approach the Needle and we snuck forward. We wanted to catch him in the act, so we waited. He had some sort of wooden stick with him, and he touched the base of the Needle with it. He was mumbling a spell, then the storm rolled in. We jumped him but he freaked, screaming about fixing things. I think Betina was against the Needle when the bolt struck."

Tony nodded. "Her body must have absorbed most of the shock. She probably saved the rest of us."

Annabel looked at Betina and Tony, her eyes shimmered with tears. "Is she going to be okay?"

"I think so, I didn't sense any permanent damage. Are you two alright?" It was a stretch to assure them Betina was fine, she'd been on the verge of very not okay when I'd gotten to her. It had felt like her flame of life was barely still flickering. I wasn't going to tell them that now though, It wouldn't help anything.

Annabel waved her hand at my concern and Tony just grunted.

"I'm fine, just burnt my hair a bit." Annabel frowned and looked down at herself. "Maybe ruined my belt." I looked at her waist and the twisted remains of her plastic belt. "I should have gone with leather tonight."

Logan was quick with the truck, and we loaded Betina in just as sirens were heard in the distance.

Spectators argued that we needed to wait, but we ignored them and hurried off. I spotted red hair and a yellow jacket among the crowd as we drove past and I almost told Logan to stop but I needed to be with Betina now, Rusty would have to wait.

Evie fussed and worried as we got Betina changed into dry clothes and tucked into her bed. Tony was going to sit with Betina until she woke, and probably for as long as she didn't yell at him to stop treating her like an invalid. Jasmine would take the couch for now, or maybe she'd join Terrance on the cot downstairs, they kept glancing at each other with hearts in their eyes.

I once again assured myself, and everyone else, that Betina was not actually dying before shooing Evie out of the bedroom so hopefully Tony would rest a bit too.

Annabel and I sat at the kitchen table with Logan and went over what happened.

"Fix it?" Logan wondered aloud. "What is he trying to fix by bringing in storms?"

I just shook my head. It didn't make sense. He was destroying our natural weather patterns over and over. "Maybe call hospitals and see if anyone came in with burns or electrical shock issues?" I suggested, even though I knew it was useless. Annabel was fine, Tony too. Likely the Warlock was unharmed if he ran off right away.

From what we could figure, Betina had absorbed the shock almost completely so it was probably safe to assume the Warlock wouldn't need any more medical attention than Annabel or Tony. I had Logan send out a few calls anyway, we had people in the hospitals, they'd watch for anyone coming in that fit the profile.

Misty swooped in with an angry flourish. She ignored everyone as she rushed to Annabel. She was clutching a patchwork bag to her chest that I hoped contained something for Betina's healing.

"What happened?" Misty demanded. She grabbed Annabel's face and looked into her eyes, humming and tisking.

"I already told you what happened and that I'm fine. Now you can see for yourself I'm fine. But Betina is not," Annabel said.

Misty pulled back and nodded sharply. "Show me to the Troll girl," she said.

"This way," I said and led Misty back to Betina's bedroom. Tony looked surprised but happy at the sight of the Witch.

Misty examined Betina's burns then pulled a salve from her bag and applied it. "This will help the healing process you started," she said to me.

I couldn't help feeling like it was a compliment of the highest order coming from her. No matter the harshness of the delivery and it gave me more confidence. Hopefully, Betina would wake in the morning feeling mostly fine. My healing abilities were new, and I wasn't sure how to use them exactly, but in those moments on the grass, I'd forced every ounce of my energy into her body, and I'd felt hers pull it in. I didn't want to tell anyone, but I think her brain was on its last loop before I'd done it and that scared the shit out of me.

Misty narrowed her lavender eyes as she finished and set the salve on the nightstand. "She can use it again in the morning then twice a day until the wounds are completely gone."

"Thank you," I said.

"My daughter has been hurt under your watch," she accused then, and I bristled.

"I would never ask Annabel to do anything outside of her ability, but this weather thing affects us all," I defended.

"So it does," she said but didn't go back on her obvious blame of me. I'd hate to think how she'd react if something serious occurred.

"Thank you for sending that idiot Elf, Gildar away. Fanlin got an earful from me for trying to set up such an obviously unequal match. Annabel is the daughter of two great clan leaders, she'll have her pick of men when she decides to conceive."

I wasn't sure how to respond to that, so I just nodded my head and watched her walk out of Betina's room.

"She's frightening," Tony whispered when she was gone.

"Very," I agreed.

Exhaustion settled over me as I accepted that everyone was going to be fine and didn't need me at the moment. More than anything, I wanted to go to bed, but I knew we had one other problem we might be able to solve tonight.

"I saw Rusty as we left the Needle," I said to the room with a resigned sigh.

"You think she's connected to the Warlock?" Logan asked.

"I don't know, but I don't trust her. It's just too weird timing."

Logan nodded. "Let's go then. Nothing more you can do here tonight."

"Not Annabel," Misty said and pushed her daughter toward the door. "Rest is what she needs, not more gallivanting with you."

I couldn't argue with that. Besides, Logan and I could handle one Magician.

Chapter Fourteen

So it was just Logan and I driving back to the hotel by the Space Needle, and I barely kept my eyes open on the way. We parked in the garage since we still had a room rented and it was likely where Anthea had tracked the rabbits the other night.

"Do we wait here for rabbits, or go up on the street and look for a redheaded Magician?" Logan asked.

"I don't know," I said honestly. "Both?"

Logan frowned at my suggestion to split up but agreed when I promised to stay in the truck and lock the doors. I even pulled out my stun gun and pepper spray just in case. I was going to observe is all, that should be safe.

I was nearly dozing off again, watching a couple rabbits hop around aimlessly when I spotted a familiar truck pull in.

"Cheating bastard," I hissed as I watched Max park in a spot across the small garage. He wasn't alone and that short black hair did not belong to his wife. I snapped a picture as discreetly as I could, but all it showed was the back of two heads. Not conclusive enough.

They sat in the truck for a few minutes, it looked like they were doing nothing more than talking, then Max got out and walked around the truck. I was laid back so low he wouldn't see me as I watched through the sideview mirror. I figured I was safe as long as he didn't recognize Logan's truck. The smile on his face made me angry and I couldn't wait to bust his ass. How dare he cheat on his wife just because she couldn't get pregnant.

He opened the passenger door and out stepped a woman who was definitely not his wife. This woman was tall and had a build similar enough to Lila to assure me she was Werewolf. I didn't recognize her as one of Logan's pack, but I knew I wouldn't recognize all of them. There were too many and I hadn't formally met every single one. I had a suspicion though that this was the woman I'd seen walk naked across the lawn with two men the other morning at Brakemoor.

I wasn't judging, at least not for that activity, this though, this was unacceptable. If she'd been there then she surely knew this man was married.

I couldn't get a good picture without being seen unfortunately, so I just watched as they walked to the elevator and once the door slid closed, I was out of the truck and rushing over to watch the floor indicator click and click. At the fourth floor it stopped. I took the stairs as fast as I could without any real plan for what to do once I got there. I just knew that I was not going to leave this hotel without the evidence needed to catch this cheater's ass.

When I rushed out onto the fourth floor, I stared down an empty hallway and frowned. I couldn't knock on every door. I needed access to room records and a keycard so I could catch them in the act. Then I could snap some pictures for evidence and maybe use the pepper spray or stun gun for good measure.

I couldn't do this alone and I still didn't want to bring Logan into it, that felt too much like a betrayal of client/P.I. confidentiality.

I called in reinforcements. Zin was happy to help and showed up twenty minutes later. Jasmine and Terrance were right behind. Jasmine was in sweats and a hoodie, looking like she'd barely rolled off the couch to get here. Terrance was looking equally as rumpled in sweats and a t-shirt. But they both had smiles and I wondered how cozy they'd been when I'd texted.

"Thank you for doing this," I said, eyeing them both suspiciously.

Jasmine blushed slightly and smoothed her hair. "Of course, we weren't doing anything anyway. Plus, how fun to be a part of your investigation!"

"Secret investigation," I reminded, eyeing Terrance who nodded.

"I can't respect this guy if he's up to what you think," Terrance said. "I'll be happy to expose him."

The statement made me like Terrance even more and Jasmine smiled up at him like she was already in love.

"Let's do this," Zin said then quickly charmed the room number from the human behind the front desk and she even managed to get a key. Vampire abilities were freaky.

She flashed me a huge smile as she held up the key and walked away from the desk leaving a very dazed looking human behind. "Let's catch the cheater," she said happily.

We took the elevator up to the fourth floor and found the door. "What's the plan?" she asked with eagerness.

"I don't want him to know he's caught just yet. So someone needs to go in and say oops. Get a feel for what they are doing and then excuse yourself saying they must have given you the wrong key and room number, no big deal."

"What if they aren't doing anything?"

"It's a hotel room and that's not his wife," I said dryly. "They aren't here to do their taxes."

"If she's pack, she'll recognize me and Terrance," Zin pointed out. "Even if *he's* new and we haven't met yet. You're sure she's Werewolf?"

"Pretty sure, yeah." Sure enough that I didn't want to risk tipping them off. "Jasmine," I said. "You're the only one they probably won't recognize in this situation." Despite Jasmine having been at Brakemoor recently, I was pretty sure neither of them would recognize her mid-coitus. Logan texted from the street. He hadn't seen Rusty or a rush of rabbits, so I told him to keep watching, all was quiet in the garage, I lied. I hated to lie to him, but I really didn't want to break Patty's trust any more than I already had involving all these extra people. I'd tell him eventually, once it was over or when I was forcing a confrontation.

If the rabbits did come into the garage, we were going to miss it, but I didn't want to walk away from this certain opportunity. If I could actually solve this one, I'd feel less like a failure all around. Rabbits and weather were next in line though.

We positioned ourselves around the hallway so we wouldn't be seen and with a big smile, Jasmine pushed into the room as if it were her own. There were screams, shouts, and apologies all around. All as I'd expected from *accidentally* walking into the wrong hotel room.

Jasmine rushed back out, letting the door close behind her with a heavy click. Her eyes were wide and her mouth gaped as she looked at me. "They, uh, they were..."

her face turned crimson. "It involved a gag and a paddle," she said quietly, hurrying away from the door.

"Oh." I was going to need bleach to get that image out of my head, but I had to ask. "Who was doing what?"

She pushed into the elevator before answering. "He's not an alpha wolf," she said meaningfully, and I barely held back a laugh.

"I could have told you that," Terrance said with a grin.

"Do you think he is just afraid to tell his wife what he likes?" Zin suggested helpfully.

"It's definitely not what she feared. There's no way he's going to impregnate her with that type of penetration," Jasmine said.

"Yikes." I really hoped that's all it was, seemed way less dramatic than what Patty had imagined. "Do I have to tell her?"

"Yes," Zin and Jasmine said in unison.

When the elevator door opened in the parking garage a frantic looking Logan was just turning from the truck, cell in hand.

"Shit," I hissed as his terrified face turned angry, taking in our little group.

"Explain," Logan demanded.

"P.I client confidentiality?" It was more a question than a statement and Logan growled then turned his eyes on Terrance.

"Don't make me take sides between my alpha and his mate," Terrance pleaded.

Logan took mercy on him and grunted looking back at me.

Terrance quickly guided Jasmine away and Zin kissed Logan's cheek then hurried off as well.

"Can we talk and drive, I'm exhausted?" I asked.

I explained it all as we drove home and although Logan didn't agree with sneaking out of the truck tonight, he agreed that I'd done the right thing in helping Patty and keeping it somewhat confidential.

"My pack needs to know they can trust you, especially when they don't feel they can come to me."

"I tried to get her to talk to you first."

"Good." He grinned at me. "I don't think I would have quite been able to discover the truth like you did though. He probably would have just admitted to cheating rather than what you just described."

I had to laugh because he was probably right. And I was going to have to explain it to Patty!

I didn't know how to tell Patty her husband wasn't just cheating, he was hiding a kinky side. There was no way I could let her keep thinking the worst though, so I sucked it up and texted her what we knew. I sent her the one picture I'd taken of the truck in the parking lot with two heads visible.

Oh my GOD! Was her response, then. *Do you know where I can pick up a strap on and some leather handcuffs?*

"Damn, Patty is into it," I said with a laugh.

Logan smiled. "Sometimes people surprise you with what they're willing to do to keep a relationship working."

I snuggled up close to him and let my eyes drift as we drove.

I went to sleep that night with one mystery solved, unfortunately it wasn't either of the mysteries that were affecting the entire city, and it wasn't going to stop the Vampires from being pissed about the wedding being ruined.

I dreamt about fangs and feelings of deep desire. There was a lot of blood and fear mixed in, making me wake up before the sun again sweating and confused as to whether or not I had been enjoying myself in the dream or not. But one thing was for certain. Dante had been playing center stage in it and that was not something I wanted to enjoy.

I rolled over and pressed myself against Logan, hoping for sleep to take me again and be dreamless. He grunted and pulled me closer. I don't think he woke up, but his protective instincts kicked in, even unconscious.

When I did fall back to sleep I dreamt of rabbits, lots and lots of rabbits.

Chapter Fifteen

Betina woke up the next day feeling tired but otherwise good. Tony kept his shop closed and sat with her all day waiting on her hand and foot. I think she enjoyed it immensely, though she'd never admit it. She prided herself on being tough. Jasmine slept half the day on the couch despite the noise of us moving around.

When she did wake up I told her about Patty's response to the kinky news.

"Good, they should be able to work things out then. It's no good hiding your desires from your partner," Jasmine said around a spoonful of peanut butter and her cheeks reddened as her eyes flicked to Terrance. He smiled at her, and it filled me with happiness to see my friend finding something good right now.

I wondered how Terrance was going to feel about Jasmine attending the wedding with Rex, and if Terrance should attend as well for security.

"Shit, I need to get a dress for Saturday," I said as thoughts of the wedding crashed into me. The wedding was quickly approaching, and I was running out of time to find a dress. I was also running out of time to solve the plagues of rabbits and weather anomalies. I looked outside at the bright sun, it was warm today, too warm. "Is it warmer than yesterday?"

"Probably," Jasmine said around her spoon of peanut butter. She'd been eating buckets of the stuff lately. She'd probably be showing in the next couple of weeks, and she was going to be the cutest pregnant lady, I was certain.

"News says the heat is setting new records the last couple days," Evie said. She was always good for a news report since she loved to watch the handsome Werewolf anchor.

Jasmine made kissy noises at Chester who was tweeting for food. He wanted her peanut butter. He swooped to her shoulder then dove for the jar. She was quick enough to dodge, then put a bit on the counter for him and sprinkled some birdseed on top. Chester hadn't cared for her at first, but they'd become friends lately, mostly because peanut butter was his favorite treat.

"The heat is coming in like a normal weather front, it's not centralized to the Space Needle or anywhere else. It can't be the Warlock's doing." I was thinking out loud, but Tony had come in for a refill on Betina's tea and stopped, looking thoughtful.

"But he said he was trying to fix something," Tony said.

"What if he's trying to fix whatever is happening with the heat? Everything he's done has been cold, he's fighting the heat wave," I gasped, connecting dots in my mind.

"Fixing it," Tony pointed out. "That means it isn't natural and someone fucked up somewhere, still could have been him."

"Maybe we're approaching this all wrong. If he's trying to fix things, he isn't the enemy, we don't need to catch him and stop him. We need to find him and maybe help him." I shrugged. "Then turn him in for fucking it up in the first place if that's what happened." I couldn't ignore the mess of all this and if he'd done something he'd need to take responsibility and punishment. But one thing at a time.

"How do you find a Warlock that doesn't want to be found?" Tony asked.

"I think I might need Logan to call in a favor with a certain news anchor," I said as a plan formed.

A couple of hours later, I was standing next to news anchor Frank Wolf, not his real name but that's what he used for his career. Not many supernaturals choose such high-profile jobs. They couldn't last too long because none of them age appropriately. Eventually Frank Wolf will have to disappear. He'd become another, *gone too soon* celebrity. I guess that's probably why he uses the fake name, easier to kill off a fake persona and start over.

"Miss Malero, thank you for joining us today to talk about your event," Frank said.

"Thanks for having me, Frank. My Yoga studio is doing a special promotion this evening. I'm inviting anyone, *weather permitting*, to work with me to *fix* whatever ails them with outdoor yoga. I am hoping that an *alliance* between us can solve the problems *plaguing* everyone. A little yoga can do a lot of good. Especially when we *work together*." I smiled at the camera, feeling like a total idiot.

Frank knew what I was doing, but everyone else was looking at me like I was nuts. The message was subtle but if the Warlock saw it, I was sure he'd understand. I wanted to work together, we could fix this weather problem together and I understood now that he wasn't the bad guy, probably. At the very least I was willing to give him the benefit of the doubt and a chance to make things right.

"That's great Miss Malero, I am sure we could all do with more yoga, and with the clear blue skies and unseasonably warm breeze, what a beautiful evening to be outside enjoying it!" He went on to give the address and important details while I smiled, and he cued the studio anchors to take over. "Subtle," he whispered with a laugh.

"Well, I hope it works."

"Me too," he agreed. "By the way, thanks for helping out my cousin the other day."

"Cousin?"

"Penelope, I'm glad she felt like she could come to the alpha's mate with such a huge thing. You're good for the pack, despite the reservations some might have over you being a Magician." He hurried away leaving me a little speechless.

Who had reservations? Probably Amber and her entire pack, but I didn't give a shit about them.

We worked for the next couple of hours to get ready for our plan. We filled the parking lot with yoga mats, brought out speakers to play soothing music, and strung up some twinkle lights.

"We should do this regularly," Sam said as she took in the effect. "I had so many calls after you were on the news and I had no idea what to tell them, thanks for giving me a heads up," she chastised.

I had forgotten that detail in my excitement. Luckily, she'd figured it out quick enough and it sounded like we were going to have a full class.

I was going to teach the class of course. Annabel, Jasmine, Terrance, and Logan would be scattered around as participants keeping an eye on things. The plan was to just watch and wait. We wanted the Warlock to approach me, we couldn't risk scaring him off again by anyone approaching him. Of course if he showed up and tried to run, we were all going to strap him down and force some answers out of him by whatever means necessary.

The crowd was big, just as Sam had predicted and as I moved through a familiar beginners yoga routine meant to stretch and relax participants, I wasn't able to spot any Warlocks. Even when I roamed around correcting postures, I didn't notice any Supes that I didn't already know.

"Nice ass," I told Logan as I adjusted his downward dog, making him growl. "Feel that stretch in your hips," I teased as I pulled him higher. "It's great for those extra energetic bedroom positions."

"I'm going to put you in this position later," he said, low enough that I barely caught it, and thankfully no human ears around would have.

"Promises, promises," I snickered and moved on so no one would guess we knew each other. I didn't want to tip off the Warlock if I could help it.

Unfortunately the class ended and I still hadn't spotted him. I was about to call it a loss when a small teenager approached me during cleanup. He had short black hair and purple eyes, this was our Warlock, I knew it. But he looked like just a kid, I wasn't expecting that. He hadn't done the yoga with us, but he must have been watching nearby.

"You're not going to arrest me, Miss Malero?" he asked hesitantly.

Logan was behind him, ready to restrain him if necessary, and Annabel was nearby in case he tried to run past me. I held up my hands and met his gaze.

"I want to help you fix whatever is going on," I said calmly.

He nodded, nervously casting his glance around and shuffling his feet. "It was an accident."

I smiled and relaxed, this was not a criminal mastermind, this was a scared kid. I could handle this. "Accidents happen. Why don't you give me a minute to clean up and we'll talk. Logan is my friend and Annabel too, I promise they won't hurt you, but they are going to watch and make sure you stick around so we can figure this out, okay?"

He flicked a fearful gaze to Logan and Annabel but nodded.

"What's your name?"

"Dexter."

"Alright, Dexter, I'm glad you came. I wasn't sure you'd get the message."

That seemed to relax him even more. "I caught it, but I wasn't sure I was going to come."

"I'm glad you did," I said.

He smiled sadly and wandered over to sit on the curb as I helped Sam clean things up. Logan hovered nearby and Annabel plopped down right next to him. She didn't engage him in conversation, they were waiting for my lead, and I appreciated that.

"Okay Dexter, let's talk," I said as we stood around a now empty parking lot.

He shuffled his feet and stuck his hands in his pockets. "My friends and I were in New Orleans, and we bought a replica Jupiter's staff."

I gritted my teeth. "Damnit Stephan, that lying bastard. It wasn't a replica," I guessed.

He shook his head. "No and we were on vacation at Cannon Beach wishing for warmer weather. It was fun to pretend we could control the weather and call in a nonstop heat wave from the tropics so we could enjoy the coast without the cold fall weather." He talked fast, tripping over his words as if he couldn't wait to get it all out.

"And it worked," I guessed.

He nodded. "None of us realized it until a couple days later when the heat kept coming and moving along the continent. Everyone freaked out and went back home to hide and pretend it wasn't us, but I knew I had to fix it."

Harsh, abandoned by his friends to fix their mess. "How old are you, Dexter?"

"Eighteen."

"Brave of you to try and fix things. Why come to Seattle though if you started this at Cannon Beach?"

"I tried to fix it there first, but on my own I wasn't powerful enough. I knew the Space Needle was an amplifier, so I came here. I thought if I called in enough cold weather fronts that it would counteract what we'd done."

"Not a bad plan," Annabel said reassuringly. "Problem is, you can't fight a spell with a spell, they just get bigger, you have to stop the one you started."

"Oh," he whispered, looking at her with googly puppy-love filled eyes.

I nearly laughed at the look; Annabel had made herself an instant admirer, I'd say.

"My coven can fix it, but we need the staff, and we need to know *exactly* what you guys said to start it," she explained.

He nodded and swallowed hard. "I think I remember."

"Don't think, know. Call your idiot friends if you have to, but it has to be right or it won't work and until then, don't use the staff. Where is it now?" Her words were clipped and harsh, but he didn't seem to care, just nodded and stared at her with those doe eyes.

"I've been staying at a motel, it's there."

"Okay, go with Annabel and get it. Then start making phone calls," I ordered.

"Yes, Ma'am," he said and jumped up, ready to follow Annabel off a cliff.

Annabel just rolled her eyes and walked off with Dexter trailing behind.

Logan put a hand on my back and leaned down to kiss my shoulder. "That's one down, almost. Good enough to not interrupt the wedding at least."

"As long as they don't mind the heat, feels like we are gaining about three degrees every day, adds up fast."

"Well, Miss yoga trainer, I was wondering if you could show me that downward dog move again. I just don't think I quite have it," he teased and grabbed my hips, pulling me back against him.

"Well, a private lesson costs big bucks."

He growled against my neck and I giggled. I loved when he got animalistic.

"Do some of your pack not approve of me as your mate?" I asked, twisting around in his arms.

The swift change of subject didn't phase him. He looked at me with a serious expression. "Some would have preferred I made a deal with Amber's father, or someone else as powerful, yes."

"And more wolfy," I said.

"Yes."

"Oh," I looked down at where our bodies touched, feeling the heat that we made together so easily. "I guess they'll just have to deal with it huh," I said, turning my face up to his with a smile, because seriously, fuck them.

His smile was enormous. "That's exactly what I told them."

He kissed me fiercely, earning a yell from Sam from across the parking lot, "Get a room!"

"Good idea," I breathed against his lips and let him pull me to his truck.

I updated my father on the drive home and he responded approvingly and also said that he wanted to meet up with the Warlock as soon as possible.

I told him not until after we got this handled, no reason to prevent a solution by jailing the perpetrator. But I did ask him to squeeze whatever information he could out of Stephan about the staff, this was as much his fault as anyone's. How the hell could he be so careless with such a powerful item? I knew the answer to that, money was all he really cared about.

Logan and I went to bed early that night, and after that private lesson he had requested, I slept like the dead curled up next to my big bad wolf. No dreams of sexy vampires tonight or rabbits.

Chapter Sixteen

Unfortunately, I woke up no closer to a solution to the rabbits, and a text from my father informing me that the blue house where we'd seen the things on our stakeout had been robbed. A diamond bracelet was missing but no one had been home the last few days so it hadn't been discovered immediately. Presumably it had happened the night we watched the rabbits congregate on their lawn, it had to be connected.

And Jasmine's father had arrived.

"Can rabbits be stealing stuff?" I wondered aloud as I poured coffee for myself and Betina. She'd stayed at Tony's last night, having felt mostly better and not wanting to take the bed from Jasmine again and make her ride the couch. More like ride Terrance, I thought by the look of satisfaction he had on his face as he sipped coffee in the kitchen.

Jasmine was still in her room, sleeping in, but I'd know it when I saw her face if they'd been getting together in the middle of the night. I was happy for my friend, Terrance was a good guy and she deserved to be taken care of and cherished because of who she is, not who her father is.

Betina had come home early this morning so she could help Jasmine and I go dress shopping for the wedding, but it seemed like that might have to be put off.

"Small stuff maybe, they're not boosting cars or anything like that," Terrance said with a laugh.

I didn't know what exactly was being stolen, but I had to imagine if it was big things that would have been specified on the news. Sophia and Jasper came in meowing for food and distracted me from my thoughts. I fed them and then Pumpkin came in to feast with her friends. Chester tweeted in behind Jasmine, hoping for peanut butter, I was sure. She avoided looking at Terrance, but her cheeks were tinged, and her smile was bright, that told me everything.

"Good morning," she said brightly and headed for the coffee.

Terrance stopped her. "Let me make you tea, it's better for the baby."

Her face flared and she giggled agreement, then hurried to busy herself getting out the peanut butter and birdseed.

"Damn," Betina whispered in my ear.

"Yep," I whispered back, behind my coffee mug. I really hated that I was going to have to ruin her happy morning. I waited until she was sitting with a hot cup of tea though. "So change of plans for today."

"Oh?" she asked with a head tilt and curious eyes.

"We need to go to my parents', your father arrived."

"Oh," she said calmly, sipping her tea.

Terrance growled and the cats scattered. Even Chester abandoned his peanut butter birdseed.

"You're not going alone, and my father is on your side as well, he just has to appear neutral. This is just a formality really," I assured her. "You aren't going to be forced to do anything."

She nodded but her hands were shaking. I couldn't imagine what she must be going through right now.

"I'll be right there with you too," Terrance assured her, touching her shoulder lightly. "In case Maddox tries anything. I'll happily eat him."

I almost rolled my eyes, as if the guise of bodyguard wasn't ruined by the looks of love in their eyes. This could go badly. It could set Maddox off and it could seriously piss off her father. I had a feeling he wouldn't approve of a love match with a Werewolf.

"I'm not sure that's a good idea," I had to point out. "If you're there, it might give Maddox reason to get more upset."

"Fuck that guy," Terrance growled. "I'm going unless Jasmine tells me she doesn't want me there. I'm not letting anyone upset her, not in her condition. She deserves better." He crouched beside her and put a finger under her chin, lifting her eyes to his. "I want to give you better," he said, and my heart just about leapt out of my chest it was so beautiful.

Betina made a gag motion, and I threw a spoon at her.

"I'd like it if you were there," Jasmine said.

I wasn't convinced it was a good idea, but I wasn't going to argue. She knew her father and Maddox better than me. Most importantly, she needed to feel safe to speak her mind and stand up for herself.

We headed to my parents' house and what was bound to be an extremely awkward conversation.

Julie, my family's longtime maid, greeted us with a stiff expression when we arrived. She'd been with my family for years and if she was on edge, I had a feeling things had gotten heated already.

When we entered the sitting room, I immediately wanted to turn around and leave. Maddox was seated next to Jasmine's father, Barnabas Goldhall, a very stern looking Magician with greying hair and tan skin. He sat stiff and regal in a black suit and silver tie. His black eyes glared at first me, and then Terrance, immediately assessing the situation. I knew he had the ability to read emotions in a room and he'd know how Terrance felt about his daughter. By the look of disgust on his face, I'd say he wasn't liking it. He should also be able to read how Jasmine felt about Maddox and Terrance. He should be able to understand that the marriage was over. He should care that his daughter was unhappy.

"Jasmine," Barnabas chastised. "Quite the trouble you've brought us all to."

He didn't care.

Terrance growled and Maddox smiled. My mother fretted next to my father. He was being careful not to touch her. She shared her feelings through touch and if my father was avoiding her, then it meant she was very unhappy, and he needed to remain calm.

I lifted my chin and stepped further into the room. I refused to be intimidated and I didn't want Jasmine to have to respond to that jackass comment. "Mr. Goldhall, it's wonderful to see you again," I said, offering my hand.

He looked annoyed at my intrusion on his chastisement but couldn't forgo the propriety of a handshake and greeting. Jasmine and Terrance settled on a couch together while I distracted Barnabas momentarily.

"I hear you're in charge of a piece of city here, Fawn, calling yourself a P.I.?" he said, and it was definitely not a compliment.

"I am," I said with a grin, ignoring the veiled insult. "It has been an adventure and I've helped so many people already. I especially enjoy how it's brought me close to so many different supernaturals," I said, knowing he was a purist who didn't believe in mixing species. "I've learned a lot about my community."

"So I hear," he grumbled.

When I finally took a seat near my parents, still clearly on Jasmine's side, Jasmine had regained her composure and was staring back at her father with a serene expression.

"I am glad you're here, Father. I have no intention of raising this child with Maddox and I fully intend to go through with the divorce. I've already begun the paperwork."

I was pretty sure she hadn't, but that was just a technicality.

Barnabas narrowed his eyes at his daughter.

"Maddox was controlling and emotionally abusive," she continued, her voice hitching a bit as she revealed what was obviously old news to her father.

He would be able to see that she had no feelings for Maddox other than fear and hatred, but so far that hadn't been enough to break the *great match*. I was more than a little disgusted by the man's actions and was thankful for the way my father stiffened at the accusations. He'd never allow such a thing to continue.

"I don't see any reason you two can't work through this trouble, women's emotions are often skewed when they are pregnant," Barnabas reasoned. "I insist you stop this nonsense and return to Florida with your husband immediately."

"Hormones! You think this is about hormones!" Jasmine exploded and I wanted to tell her to keep it together because if she didn't, she was going to prove him right and things would not go easy.

"What else would drive you back to a town where you had an affair with some *girl* then turn around when she isn't available and chase a Werewolf's tail?" Barnabas motioned at Terrance who looked ready to shift and attack.

Oh shit. I stared at Jasmine, refusing to look and see if my parents were connecting those dots or not.

"Everyone needs to calm down," my father ordered.

Barnabas was red faced and fuming, Terrance looked like he wanted to rip someone's head off and tears were streaming down Jasmine's face. My empathetic drive was coursing through me and it was difficult not to pull her in for a hug I knew she desperately needed.

Maddox looked satisfied with Jasmine's sadness and I wanted to throw something at him. He was lucky I had left my stun gun in the car. He thought he could bully her into doing what he wanted and had brought along a bigger bully to help.

"I'll forgive her indiscretions," Maddox said magnanimously, and I scoffed.

"I deserve to be happy," Jasmine whispered and grabbed Terrance's hand. "I deserve someone who treats me like I matter, who knows that I'm more than my family name and power."

"You never complained when I was buying you jewelry and taking you on trips," Maddox snapped. "This is ridiculous, you will return to me now."

"Fuck you. You can keep the jewelry, Maddox, I left it behind anyway. I took nothing you ever gave me."

"Except that!" He pointed at her belly. "You stole my seed and ran off. I demand you return it."

Jasmine gasped and protected her belly, Terrance put a possessive hand over her stomach as well and I saw a fight coming if someone didn't step in with a reasonable voice.

I hoped it would be my father and not me, I wasn't sure I could speak without yelling at the idiocy of Maddox's statement.

"What the fuck are you suggesting," Terrance demanded.

"She needs to stay with me until the pregnancy ends. Then she can leave, and she will *not* be taking the child with her. If she doesn't want anything I've given her, she doesn't want the child." Maddox spoke like a spoiled brat and even Barnabas gave him a frustrated look. Apparently, this wasn't part of their plan.

Jasmine was speechless, her mouth gaped, and she stared at Maddox. Barnabas said nothing. Maddox's lip quirked up in a smile thinking he'd just won.

It took everything I had not to lash out. This wasn't my fight to win, but I was damn sure not going to stand by and let Jasmine lose. I looked at my father but he was keeping his expression blank. Not my mother, she looked ready to burst into tears.

I needed to do something, if Maddox wanted the baby, likely because of the possibilities of its powers, then that's where I needed to target.

"How do you know it's yours," I challenged casually and threw a meaningful look at Terrance.

He caught on immediately. "It's my child, I went to Florida and met secretly with her, that is why she returned here to Seattle. It is why she and I have such a strong obvious connection now. You don't think we fell in love in a mere day," he laughed. "We have been having an affair for years."

Jasmine turned her shocked expression on Terrance.

I knew no one in the room believed the story, but there was no way to prove he was wrong, at least not before the baby came out and had zero Werewolf abilities.

Then again, halflings didn't always present with both parents' abilities. Maybe it was the perfect plan.

No one spoke for a full minute as the implications of his words sunk in. I was looking for holes in his claim and saw plenty, but it would work to buy time I was sure. Maybe that would be enough to get a more legal and final plan in place.

I could back him up. "That's why Logan and I have vowed to protect her as one of our pack," I said. "She carries the child of one of ours," I offered as further proof. "Logan has put her under his protection. He told Maddox as much when he showed up at my house and threatened her and me."

My parents looked at me with surprise, I'd never claimed Logan's pack as my own, though they were aware of our relationship. This was all getting very complicated.

"You threatened my daughter?" my father asked with a deadly calm that even gave me a chill.

Maddox had the self-preservation instincts to spit and stutter an apology and excuse of only trying to get to Jasmine, it hadn't been a serious threat.

It reminded me that I needed to get Annabel to redo the wards around the house when she was fully healed, no one was protected there at the moment.

Barnabas looked at Maddox. "Is this true?" He wasn't asking about threatening me or his daughter, he only wanted to know if she was under the pack's protection.

Maddox just shrugged, he couldn't deny it. Logan had definitely claimed her, put her under his protection, he'd just never said anything to indicate the baby was pack.

"And Logan will back up this story?" Barnabas asked with annoyance.

"Of course he will," I said, and I knew it was true because Logan would do anything I asked of him, within reason, and protecting an innocent child was definitely within reason.

"It's not true! I was sleeping with my wife and that baby could still be mine despite who else she whored around with," Maddox whined.

Terrance growled fiercely and my father stiffened, ready to intervene and keep the peace if necessary. Violence would not be tolerated.

Barnabas gave Maddox a look that clearly said *shut up*. "Nothing will be done until the child is born. It will be simple enough to discern the father at that time," Barnabas said, giving Maddox a meaningful look.

Maddox huffed and crossed his arms, "Well, I'm not leaving town until that's done," he warned darkly. "I won't be tricked out of a powerful heir."

We had bought Jasmine time was all. A few months and she'd be forced to prove who the father was.

Jasmine's lips were a thin line and her body was held so stiff she was shaking. Even Terrance's hand on her back didn't seem to soothe her at all. "I still want a divorce, our child or not, I am not staying married to you," she stated with a finality that had her father widening his eyes in surprise. I would bet she's never really stood up for herself before.

Good for her.

"That seems quite fair," my father said and looked at Barnabas expectantly. "We can't control the hearts of our children, the best we can do is hope they make choices to end up with a happy life."

"It's not her heart I need to control," Barnabas gritted out. "I will not support this. I may not be able to stop you from making this decision, but I won't support it. You will not have access to your inheritance, you are cut off, Jasmine, how will you survive without the luxuries you are so accustomed to?" he sneered with satisfaction.

"*He* can't provide for you the way Maddox can." He jutted his chin toward Terrance disdainfully. "Neither can *she*," he sneered in my direction.

Terrance growled and I glared.

"We take care of our pack," I said and notched my chin up. Out of the corner of my eye I saw a smile of satisfaction on my mother's face. "She has a job and a place to live, she doesn't need to sell herself or her womb to Maddox or you, for anything more."

"This is ridiculous!" Maddox snapped but Barnabas held up his hand, not breaking eye contact with me.

"Fine, Jasmine wants to stay with the *dogs*, I see that's what the Magicians around here do."

My father frowned and I could tell he was about to lose his well contained composure. Barnabas was a friend of his, but coming into his territory and insulting the way he ran it and his family, that would be unacceptable.

"I think it's best if you leave," my father said calmly and he didn't just mean the house, he wanted Barnabas out of town and that made me smile even wider.

Barnabas startled and looked at my father, quickly covering his annoyance. "Yes, I see there's no reason for me to be here. Maddox, give her the divorce, but stay in town. When the baby comes." He looked at his daughter with hate in his eyes. "Check it. If it's a full Magician, I want it."

Jasmine huddled closer to Terrance as her father and future ex-husband were led out by my father.

My mother moved to sit close to me, she embraced me, and I was instantly flooded with worry and surprisingly, pride. I embraced her back, letting her flood me with emotions. When she pulled back there were tears in both our eyes.

"You're doing good things here," she whispered. "But make sure that Jasmine is prepared for what will happen when that baby comes out."

I nodded.

"I won't let them take anything from her," Terrance growled and my mother smiled at him warmly.

When my father came back, Julie brought in a tea tray and cookies. I slipped away as everyone tried to eat and nibble and talk about anything that didn't have to do with the conversation we'd just had.

I needed to talk to Stephan while I was here. I knew my father had already questioned him about the staff and likely there wasn't anything helpful because he hadn't bothered to let me know the result, but I wanted to hear for myself what he knew about the thing.

I walked downstairs and past empty cells with bars unbreakable by manpower or spell. My father had a unique ability to forge steel that could hold any Supe, it's why he could control such a large area for so long. Why even Barnabas was forced to respect him.

Regardless of the futility, I knew Stephan was trying to get out, Betina's twin brother had been down here recently and said the Magician muttered spells at night, but so far, he'd been unable to do a damn thing and it made me extremely happy.

When his usefulness was done, he'd be put to death, it was the punishment for selling so many magical items to humans. The risk to all of us was great, all for greed. He couldn't be trusted.

He was sitting on his cot today, black slacks and shiny shoes, a red button up unbuttoned enough to show gold chains at his chest. His hair was slicked back, and he looked like he'd recently shaved. His black eyes assessed me with a smirk.

I hadn't dressed up for this. I was wearing black shorts and a purple tank top because the weather was again far too hot for October. My tall purple boots added a helpful flair making me feel confident in my skin. But he knew the best way to get to me was to silently judge what I was wearing so he raised an eyebrow as he met my gaze again.

"Well, I wondered when I'd be seeing you again. With the odd weather I've been hearing about, I'm surprised it took so long." He wrinkled his nose. "And is that poop on your shoe?"

I looked down and frowned, it was definitely rabbit poop, great.

"I've been busy," I drawled, leaning against the bars of the empty cell opposite Stephan's. "What do you know about it all? Sell a staff to a few kids as if it weren't anything special?"

He huffed a laugh. "What do you know so far?"

"Kids bought a staff at a shop in New Orleans, thought it was a replica of Jupiter's Staff, turns out they were able to call in a heat wave and now one of them is trying to fix it with storms."

"Heat wave? Julie has only been telling me about snow and ice storms," he said casually.

I bristled at the mention of Julie, why the hell was she down here conversing with Stephan? I was going to have to mention that to my father.

"What do you know about the staff, was it sold in your shop?"

"I already told your father, we never would have sold a real magical item for the price of a replica."

I rolled my eyes. Of course, it was all about money with him, he didn't care about selling magical items, he cared about getting the right price for it. I actually believed him.

"Who else is selling this stuff?"

He shrugged. "If it was someone who didn't know what it really was, it had to have been a human."

"So how did they get the real Jupiter's staff?"

"You think all of the magical items throughout history have been kept out of human hands until I came along willing to sell them?" he scoffed. "Don't be stupid, Fawn."

"Fuck you, Stephan, you're very close to losing your usefulness and a thick rope is at the end of it," I threatened.

He laughed as if he couldn't care less, but I didn't miss the quick way he touched his neck. "Wielding the power of the staff is nothing intricate, why do you need my help?" he said accusingly, trying to cover his apprehension.

"Because the idiot Warlock who did the spell doesn't remember how he did it."

Stephan laughed. "And you think selling magical items to humans is bad. Giving them to untrained supernaturals is worse because they have the innate power to do real damage."

"So, what do you know about controlling the thing?" I let my frustration show and his eyes glinted with enjoyment. His biggest joy now was feeling important, which is why he was so slowly dolling out information on the items he'd sold.

He looked at his nails. "Not much, only rumors. I imagine you've already got the witches working on it?"

I nodded.

"They'll know as much as me."

Maybe he really didn't know, which is probably why my father hadn't bothered to update me on his conversation with the prisoner. "What do you know about rabbits?" I asked, giving up on help with the weather issue.

"Rabbits? As in Easter and lucky feet?"

"Something like that, yeah." Apparently, the rabbit issue hadn't made it into Julie's pillow talk. I hoped it wasn't pillow talk. I was fairly certain Julie had no way to get into his cell so anything they were doing would be extremely inventive and made standing here in front of his cell very uncomfortable.

"They aren't inherently powerful in any way, not particularly dangerous. Are you thinking of getting a pet, want to start up an act and pull one out of a hat, Fawn?"

"Useless," I mumbled and walked away. "Your days are numbered, Stephan."

"They certainly are," he said so quietly I wasn't sure I heard him correctly.

No closer to a solution but with a brand new problem, I asked my father to talk to me in his office.

"Julie's been talking to Stephan."

"She delivers his meals."

"What if its more?"

He looked thoughtful. "I'll talk to her. She's been with us for years, I trusted her to help raise all my children. Why would she throw that away on a death row inmate?"

"Maybe he offered her something she couldn't refuse?"

"Like what?"

I wanted to say a good roll in the sack, but this was my father I was talking to. "A chance at romance? Or a magical item?" She was a rare Magician born without any powers and although she seemed happy enough with her life, I could imagine it irked her to live amongst so many magical beings and be basically human.

He straightened up and his face became more serious. "I'll speak with her."

"Thanks," I said.

"I like the way you're handling things with Jasmine. It's not the way things have been done in the past, but I can't imagine letting my daughter continue in an unhappy relationship, especially if it were in any way abusive."

"Thank you," I said with a huge grin. I knew my father loved me but hearing him approve of me shaking things up gave me the confidence to keep doing it. It reminded me of the way I was changing Logan's pack. I liked knowing I was making a better world for supernatural women everywhere. Maybe that's what my father envisioned when he put me in charge of a part of Seattle in the first place, it had certainly been an unconventional placement for a daughter.

I should have been married off, much like Jasmine had been.

Chapter Seventeen

When we left my parents' house, I didn't know what to say to Jasmine and Terrance about their situation. So I didn't. They sat close in the car, and I was happy for them. Meanwhile, I feared for what would happen in seven months when a full Magician baby was born.

Terrance must have texted Logan to let him know what the story was because Logan sent me a message saying he was happy to have a new member in his pack. I think he was just happy he didn't have to worry about Jasmine trying to reignite her relationship with me.

We picked Betina up at the house so we could do our dress shopping and Jasmine filled her in on what had happened.

"Hey," Betina said, leaning over the backseat. "What if we get Annabel to curse that baby?"

"What!" Jasmine and I said in unison.

"Not like a curse curse, just like a doesn't smell like a Magician when it's born type of curse. It doesn't even have to smell like Werewolf, it's just got to not be full Magician, could be half human for god's sake. Maybe Jasmine was a total slut a few months ago."

"Magicians can't breed with humans," Jasmine mumbled but she didn't argue the total slut part and I thought that was promising. Better to be a slut then permanently tied to an asshole.

"Okay, so not half human, but you get what I mean," Betina said.

I did, and I didn't think it was a terrible idea. It would be tricky to keep up on though through the child's lifetime. Luckily it wasn't my baby, and it wasn't pertinent to the next few months.

The car was silent the rest of the drive.

"Did you hear anything from Annabel this morning about the staff?" Jasmine asked as we entered a shop with bridal gowns and prom dresses.

"She got the staff last night and took Dexter to the coven house. He's written down everything he remembers from the night they did the original spell, but they aren't going to try to reverse it until he confirms with a few of his buddies. So they're waiting for them to get back to him, I guess. At least the staff is safe until then and the coven is making sure he has someone with him at all times, so he doesn't make a run for it." I laughed. "Not that I think that's going to be a problem, Annabel said he follows her around like a lost puppy with heart eyes and tells her how beautiful she is at least once an hour. Poor kid is destined for a broken heart."

"Awe," Jasmine cooed. "Love is so wonderful, especially young love." She looked at me with a soft smile and I knew she was remembering our own young love. Then her eyes glanced to Terrance who was looking uncomfortable in a white and gold chair.

"New love is great at any age," I said with a smile.

She sighed heavily. "Yeah, it is, isn't it." Happy tears filled her eyes. "I don't deserve what he's offered me," she whispered.

I pulled her into my arms, and she sniffled on my shoulder. "Yes, Jasmine, you do," I assured her and stroked her back while giving Terrance a look that indicated we were fine. He sat back down but didn't take his eyes off of us. He was so protective. "You're a good person, Jasmine."

"I did cheat on him," she admitted.

"He's an asshole, I would have cheated on him too. But does that mean this might not be his baby for real?" I asked, indicating her stomach.

"No, it was with a human. A beautiful woman with light brown hair and dark eyes," she whispered and kissed my nose before excusing herself to use the bathroom.

I ignored the little flair of... jealousy? Excitement? Whatever it was and turned to a rack of dresses.

Terrance followed, hovering outside the door and when she emerged, he hugged her tight and kissed her deeply.

"Damn those two make me miss Tony," Betina said.

"Weren't you with him last night," I laughed.

"Yeah, but still, look at that."

I did, and I agreed. It made me miss Logan too.

We tried on dress after dress, some more practical than others just for fun. I was pretty sure I was going to wear black to the wedding. Not because I didn't approve, but because I knew it was Anthea's favorite color and I looked good in it.

I turned in front of Jasmine in a gold party dress that barely covered my ass but came up in a turtleneck style with long sleeves and a back that reached my panty line.

"Yes! If you wear that dress then Logan won't be able to keep his tongue in his mouth," Jasmine teased.

"If you wear that outside, you'll get arrested for solicitation," Betina snickered.

I turned in the mirror and had to agree with both statements. It was a bit much for a wedding, but damn, I looked hot and cheap.

"I'm trying this one. Terrance come with me so you can get my zipper," Jasmine said with a seductive wiggle of her hips as she held up a shimmering red floor length gown.

Terrance followed her happily and Betina flipped through racks for something else I should try.

My attention was caught by a flash of red hair out the shop window. Black eyes, yellow jacket tied around her waist and green backpack straps visible. She stood there staring at me and winked before she started moving through the crowd. I knew she'd be swallowed up and disappear if I didn't act immediately. I wondered briefly if I was rushing into a trap. But I didn't care, I wasn't going to let her get away.

I ran out of the store, the shouts of the shop girls didn't deter me, Jasmine and Betina would reassure them, or pay them. Maybe I *would* wear this to the wedding.

I'd already lost Rusty among the crowd moving along but I wasn't giving up. She was my best shot at solving the rabbit infestation, I was more sure than ever.

The crowd was thick today and she'd been moving with it so I followed along throwing elbows until she was right there in front of me.

"Hey," I shouted. "Rusty." I needed to be sure this time, no more fender benders without good cause.

She turned and her black gaze met mine then she turned and started to run, but I wasn't going to lose her this time. Unfortunately I wasn't wearing shoes and that gave her a clear advantage. She wasn't pulling away though. She was staying in sight as she moved.

On purpose?

"Stop!" I demanded with enough force that others looked at me as if I had some kind of authority, which they quickly dismissed when they took in my outfit. "Stop her! The redhead," I shouted hoping someone would help before questioning whether or not they should. I probably looked like a hooker trying to chase down a John who hadn't paid. I hit a rock with my foot and nearly toppled but managed to stay up by grabbing a stranger for balance. The woman looked at me like I had leprosy and brushed my touch off, sure it was going to stain her pink shirt.

I glared at her and ran, hobbling only slightly. "Fucking stop!"

Rusty took a sharp turn, ducking into a street level parking garage. I followed but it was dark inside and there was no sign of her anywhere.

"What the hell?" I grumbled. There was no way I was going to walk down every aisle searching for her. "I don't know why you're running, I just want to talk and I think you want to talk to me too," I shouted into the darkness. My voice echoed around the garage and a few rabbits hopped about. I watched them with annoyance. Were they robbing people under Rusty's orders?

I yanked my skirt down wondering how many people had gotten a free glimpse of my ass as I'd run down the street. I leaned against a car and pulled my hurt foot up. It was bleeding, great.

"Come on. Let's talk," I called out, loath to keep searching in this condition. It was going to be hard enough to walk back to the dress shop.

I started moving further into the garage then felt a brush of something behind me. I turned with a jerk, reaching for my nonexistent pepper spray or stun gun as I bumped into a large muscular chest and a mumbled word later, everything went black.

I woke up slowly, brain foggy and eyes unwilling to adjust. My foot hurt and I started to remember what I'd been doing.

"I think she's waking up," a feminine voice said.

"About time," a gruff male said.

"Who are you," I asked groggily, trying to force my eyes to focus on the two blobs swimming in my vision. I thought I recognized one of the voices. "Rusty?"

"How the hell does she know your name Rust?" The male growled.

"I met her on the street a few days ago. Didn't realize she'd be such a problem."

"You're getting careless in your old age, babe."

"Fuck you, Allen!"

"What is a prostitute doing chasing you anyway, and in the middle of the day?" Allen stepped closer and peered down at me. He got close enough that I was able to focus. He was a big man; I would have mistaken him for a Werewolf if it wasn't for the unmistakable black eyes. He was a magician. His blond hair was pulled back in a ponytail and he had three gold hoops in his left ear. He was wearing a tight black tank top and jeans. Sweat dripped down his cheek and neck and I became aware that wherever we were, it was blazing hot. He wiped his forehead before stepping back. "A Magician prostitute?"

"I'm not—" I began but Rusty was suddenly leaning over me and there was a warning on her face that made me bite back the denial.

"She likes me. I guess I look like her type. How the hell should I know, but you grabbed her and now she's here, this is on you, Allen, not me."

What was she playing at? I didn't trust her, but Allen looked like he'd like to break me in half and throw me in the sound rather than deal with a prisoner, so I kept my mouth shut.

"I wasn't sure if she was a problem, better to deal with out of sight. But now that I see what she is, maybe we can ransom her before we move on. Take a vacation. A Magician usually has family, even a powerless one who's walking the streets for money."

"I told you, we don't deal in people," Rusty snapped. "For the last time, we are grab and go, small trinkets, easy sell and that's it." Rusty was standing in front of me, hands on hips and looking at Allen.

My head was settling, and my vision was almost back to normal. I wanted to sit up, but wasn't sure my head could take it so I just glanced around at my surroundings as they argued about the best use of their criminal time in Seattle. We were in a small space, all concrete and most terrifying, no doors. I searched everywhere I could see, walls, ceiling, floor; not a door in sight, what the hell was going on?

"Well now she's here, you expect me to just let her go?" Allan snapped.

"No," Rusty said, much to my disappointment. "At least, not yet." She glanced back at me with an apologetic look. "We can finish up our game here and let her loose when we move on."

"Or now, now's good and I promise not to say anything to anyone," I said and sat up. My head spun as I did, and I was certain for a second that I was going to puke.

"Not a chance," Allen huffed. "I'm going out for food, don't let her out while I'm gone, Rusty, or I'll snap your neck."

"Whatever," Rusty grumped and plopped down in a chair obviously used to his threats.

Allen walked to a wall and then through it. I blinked for an entire minute as I tried to wrap my head around *that*. The man had just walked through the fucking wall. "What," I finally gasped.

"As if I could let you out even if I wanted to," Rusty sighed. "Obviously." She motioned to the space Allen had stepped through, no indication that it wasn't solid.

I looked at her with wide eyes and she just shook her head.

"We are in a tomb, sealed from the outside and he's the key."

"A tomb?" I jumped up and looked down at the *table* I'd been lying on, it was a damn sarcophagus. I really *was* going to puke now. "Oh my god."

"I know, it creeped me out at first too, but it's really not that bad, at least it's quiet." Rusty shrugged.

"Dead people tend to be that way." I wasn't sure what to do with myself, so I leaned against a wall and crossed my arms, assessing the situation. I couldn't exactly arrest her, I didn't have any cuffs in this dress and if Allen came back and he realized who I was, then I might be in real trouble.

I needed out before I made a move against her. But, we were locked in, sealed in. There were a couple folding chairs, the *not table*, and that was it. "You guys aren't living here," I pointed out.

"No, we stay in hotels, but this is our safe space for when Allen gets scared."

"By what?"

She looked embarrassed. "When Allen gets paranoid, I get stashed away. I never know what is going to set him off."

"You're his prisoner." I stood up and gaped, if she was his prisoner too, then how the hell was I going to get out of here?

She just shrugged. "Like I said, when he gets paranoid. We don't usually stay in one place so long but he's settled in here, likes how productive our time has been. People are starting to get suspicious though, people and Supes. Obviously the abnormal number of rabbits isn't going unnoticed."

"So you *are* responsible for them, huh? I had a feeling."

She nodded and had the decency to look embarrassed.

"What's wrong with them? They don't talk to me. Well, the one you were holding the first time we met did, but the rest, nothing."

Her eyes widened. "It's true, you talk to animals? I wasn't sure, but I hoped."

"It's one of my abilities," I said vaguely, not wanting to give away too much.

"Peter is the one that talked to you, but the others can't because they're dead," she explained casually.

I could have guessed a hundred things and that wouldn't have been one of them. I stared at her like she had just grown a second head hoping she'd show a sign that she was joking. She didn't. Zombie rabbits? This was not something I knew how to deal with and it gave me the creeps. But some things started to make sense. Dead animals wouldn't be afraid of a predator like Logan and they could be attracted to other dead things, like Evie.

"You are bringing rabbits back from the dead? To steal?" I was having Ben flashbacks and it wasn't pleasant.

I could almost smell the formaldehyde and depression that had permeated his mom's basement. Not to mention the Lysol and fragrant candles covering the smell of her dead body in the living room.

"Peter did."

"Your pet rabbit is resurrecting his friends?" I gasped; not sure I wasn't still in the middle of a magic induced dream. I half expected Dante to show up and save me while pulling me in for a passionate kiss. If only I could force myself to wake up.

"Peter is not my *pet!* I love Peter." Her face reddened and she looked at her feet. "He is my fiancé."

I had to sit down at that information, and I suddenly didn't care that it was on the top of a dead guy inside of a tomb.

"He wasn't always a rabbit," she explained. "He was a Magician with the ability to shapeshift into a rabbit."

"Rare," I said quietly, but I'd heard of other shapeshifters, it was like Anthea's ability to turn into a bat. It happened, but not a lot.

"Yes, quite rare and he also has the ability to, well for lack of a better term, *zombify* things."

"So the rabbits running around the city are dead, you guys brought them here to steal…" I trailed off, not sure where to even go with that thought.

"It was Allen's idea, he can call to them."

"The rabbits?"

She nodded, "Dead things that have been resurrected." She took a shaky breath. "They are twins, each with half the ability. Peter raised them from the dead and Allen controls them. Without Peter able to send them back to their natural state, Allen is unstoppable."

"Wow." I'd heard of this happening in twins before, it was actually quite common for them to have similar or linked abilities. I've never heard of anything this morbid of course. "But Peter is stuck now?"

"I don't know what happened. The three of us had been going around the country, town to town on a small scale stealing and moving on." Shame filled her eyes and she fidgeted. She was admitting to quite the offense. "Peter went out with the herd one day and when Allen called them back, he just never shifted and the rabbits stayed animated." Tears stung her eyes, and she shuffled her feet. "I lured you into that garage because I was hoping you could help me. I know you're in charge of Seattle. I didn't know for sure that you could talk to animals though. I think that could really help us."

"You want my *help?*" I crossed my arms over my chest and raised an eyebrow. "Kidnapping me isn't exactly the best way to ask for help, Rusty."

She met my gaze with contrition. "I know, but what else could I do? I didn't expect Allen to be prowling around in the garage when I ducked in. That was just bad luck."

"For both of us apparently," I grumbled.

"I think Allen did something to Peter. I can't let him know I'm trying to get your help with it, I would have found myself locked in a tomb."

"As opposed to this," I snapped.

She gave me an apologetic look. "I'm desperate," she admitted. "Peter was always the one who kept Allen in check, never letting things get this out of hand. Since he's been stuck as a rabbit, Allen's gotten bolder and bolder, and I don't know what he might do next. If I just take Peter and leave, I'm afraid he'll find us, and Peter is defenseless as he is."

My empathy was kicked in full gear now and outweighing my own self-preservation. There was no way

I could turn her down, she was desperate and in need. *Damnit*, I had to help her and her little rabbit too.

"I'll try to help, but you'll all have to answer for your crimes, Rusty. You can't just go around stealing."

"I know," she said with tears in her eyes. "I would rather see Peter in a cell beside me than stuck in this form and controlled by Allen forever."

And Allen definitely needed to pay for his crimes. If he'd done something to keep his brother in rabbit form, that was serious.

"Where is Peter now?" I asked.

"Out with the other rabbits. When Allen returns, I'll convince him to let you go, and then tonight you can meet me at the Space Needle. There's a hotel parking lot next to it with a drain leading to the sewer. That's where Allen calls them back, where they deliver their goods."

"That's why they went in and disappeared," I said, surprising her.

"How did you know?"

"A friend followed them the other night. I don't know why we never thought of looking for a path into the sewer.

Rusty frowned. "I can't believe Allen didn't notice he was followed, he's so careful all the time, paranoid."

I wasn't going to explain that it had been a vampire bat following, no need to reveal any secrets that might be needed later. "We went back during the day and my Witch friend couldn't sense anything off. I'm surprised she couldn't find the residue of whatever magic he is using to call them to him."

Rusty smiled. "That's me, I can hide magic."

Great, a Magician outside the law and able to cover her tracks. If Rusty changed her mind and decided she didn't want my help, I'd never find her again, I was sure.

We fell into silence, and I tried to think up a plan because I had little faith in her ability to get Allen to just let me go, even if he did think I was a prostitute. Then I was going to need to figure out how to help her fiancé who is currently stuck as a rabbit and arrest them all for theft too.

My life was never boring.

Chapter Eighteen

Allen returned about an hour later looking angry and carrying a bag of fast food. He walked through the wall like it didn't exist and I was tempted to run at the spot and see if the lingering magic would let me out. But I didn't want to end up with a bloody nose to match my bloody foot, or stuck somewhere inside the wall, half in and half out of the tomb.

Allen eyed me skeptically and held out a bag.

"I'm a vegetarian," I said with a frown.

"Fries then," Allen said and took the burger out and handed me the bag again.

I was thankful for a little sustenance and scarfed them down. If I had to fight my way out, a little strength would be needed. We ate in silence and Allen watched me the whole time in a way that made me incredibly uncomfortable. I started to worry he was going to make me prove I was a prostitute in order to gain my freedom. I'd rather wait here until Logan found me or I died of starvation. Logan would have to find me eventually, wouldn't he? His Werewolf nose was pretty good.

Unfortunately he'd have no idea where to start looking and the city was big.

I looked over at the thick wall beside me. No telling how much concrete stood between me and the chance that Logan could catch my scent in here.

"Can we let her go now? We need to get out there soon, the sun is setting," Rusty said as she finished her burger.

Shit, was it really that late?

"So she can run off and tattle on us? No, she stays until we finish here. She'll be free to go when we move on."

"Fuck, how long is that going to take because I'm going to need to make some phone calls," I grumped. At least he wasn't talking about killing me.

"A few days," Allen said with an unapologetic smile.

"Well you better take me somewhere else for a few days, because I'm not doing my business in a bucket in front of you two," I snapped as if that was the biggest concern to this entire situation.

Rusty barely covered a laugh behind her water bottle and Allen darted a glare her way.

"She's got a point, Allen. You can't expect her to stay here for a few days, let's just take her to the hotel."

"They better have cable," I whined, trying my best to play the part of kidnapped prostitute. "Pretty Woman is always on cable."

Allen sighed heavily. "Fine." He stalked across the distance and leaned down until his face was just a breath from mine. "I don't trust you, Magician," he whispered. Then his voice deepened, and his words were a blur as I slumped into blackness.

When I woke again, I was in a familiar hotel room and cuffed securely to the bed.

"Damn," I hissed as I pulled and the sharp metal bit into my wrist.

"Sorry, I tried to convince him it wasn't necessary, but he wouldn't listen. Like I said, paranoid," Rusty explained.

"And how am I supposed to use the bathroom?"

Her face heated and she looked away. "Um, well Allen took you in before he cuffed you, he woke you up just enough to follow orders and do what was necessary. You should be okay until he gets back."

Wow, I could have lived without knowing that. I felt violated and there was no way I was going to keep playing along with a man who had those kinds of supernatural abilities. He needed to be locked up in my father's basement. Though the idea of him and Stephan trading secrets was a bit terrifying too.

"I need to get out of here."

"I know, I promise I'll do whatever I can. When he falls asleep tonight, I'll grab the keys and—"

"No, fuck that. I'll talk to your rabbit but I'm not playing along as prisoner to that psychopath. Give me your cell, I'm calling for help. You're welcome to leave before they get here so they don't kill you, but that's it, that's all I'm offering." My tone left no room for argument, and it was clear that if she didn't give me her phone to make the call, she was not going to have me on her side to talk to Peter.

Her face filled with worry, and she clutched her hands in front of her. "He'll kill me if he comes back and you're gone, he'll know I helped you."

I couldn't believe this woman, she was asking me to just lay here and let Allen control me, knock me out and who the hell knew what else he would decide to do.

"Hard pass, give me your phone."

She pulled a phone from her pocket and stood up, but she didn't come closer. "Please, please help me stop him and get Peter back."

"I can't help you from here, Rusty." I kept my voice calm, but it was difficult. "Let me make a call and I will do what I can. Go, find Peter, and meet me at my house. Allen doesn't have to know you've helped me until it's too late." I managed not to show it but inside, I was freaking out, there was no guarantee Allen would be gone long enough for me to get someone here to help. It was dark outside, and I had to assume he was out there controlling the rabbits, sending them in after whatever it was he wanted, gold and jewelry I assumed. "Your help here is going to go a long way when it comes to sentencing," I added as a last-ditch effort to get her to agree.

"I am so sorry for all of this," she said.

I believed her, I could tell she was scared and it made me want to help her. "I know, now help me by dialing, will you?"

She nodded and came forward. I scooted up the bed far enough to reach my ear to my hand. Her eyes were full of worry and fear, that's how I knew I was doing the right thing. The really bad people, truly evil people, they couldn't get that deep of feeling into their eyes. Their souls just didn't shine like that. Rusty had made some bad decisions and found herself in a terrible situation, but she deserved a little hand out of the pit she'd dug. Allen probably didn't.

I gave her the only number I knew by heart and she dialed, then handed me the phone. "Hi dad."

It wasn't even twenty minutes before they started to arrive. My dad hadn't wasted any time, he called in everyone he could.

Anthea was first, her bat abilities really made travel through the city at night easy. She fluttered to the window but couldn't get in. Rusty had left right after I'd given my dad the pertinent information and I was still cuffed to the bed. I couldn't open the window for her, but just seeing her there flitting happily was relief enough, I was going to be okay.

Howls pierced the night next, and I knew Logan and his pack were on the way. But the one who busted in the door was a surprise.

"A more beautiful site has never met my eyes," Dante hissed with a wicked grin as his gaze ravished my body. The short dress had hiked up a bit and I was certain he caught sight of my black thong.

I didn't care though; I was so happy to see him I would have willingly admitted to all the dirty things he'd pushed into my dreams if he'd just cross the room and uncuff me.

"Get me out of here," I demanded as he took his time crossing the room.

"It would be my pleasure," he drawled, leaning over, and snapping the cuffs with such ease I shivered at the show of strength.

"Thank you," I whispered as I rubbed my wrists and sat up. "We should get out of here before Allen returns."

Dante nodded and scooped me up. We were out the door and into the hallway before I could even register to complain.

"I can walk," I snapped but he only smiled, flashing a bit of fang.

"I know, but it is a good excuse to hold you tight. Besides, you aren't wearing any shoes and I can smell you've had a bleeding cut that's barely scabbed over."

I had no response for that, so I let him carry me until we were inside the elevator, then I demanded release and he reluctantly agreed.

"Thank you," I said as the elevator headed down. "I wasn't expecting you."

"I'm glad your father thought to call me." His gaze traveled down my body again and I pulled on the skirt, hoping for a little modesty.

"I was thinking this might be too much for the wedding," I said to break the heated silence.

He grunted. "It is very... provocative. I would worry that too many eyes would be on you in that dress. Best to show less skin and more personality I think."

I was surprised by that statement and couldn't help laughing. "Sounds like something my father would say."

He leaned down just as the first floor dinged. "I am thinking very unfatherly thoughts about you, as always," he whispered in my ear making me shiver. His breath was hot and sweet and brought back memories of our kiss. I would never forget what he tasted like.

When the doors opened, I practically ran from the small space, needing air that didn't smell like him.

Anthea was there to greet us in someone's stolen jacket that barely covered her ass. She hurried forward to embrace me. "I saw you, I found you first," she cheered and winked at me. "Daddy was second."

"Thanks," I said and a howl drew my gaze to the front doors where three large Werewolves paced, and one very naked man stood glaring and panting.

"Logan," I cried and rushed out to him while the front desk clerk shouted for someone to call the police.

His arms were around me an instant later and I let the tension leave my body.

"Damnit Fawn, what the hell happened?" he demanded.

"Take me home and I'll tell you on the way," I said with a sigh. I wanted out of this dress, and I wanted shoes.

"She was handcuffed to the bed," Anthea said helpfully.

Logan trembled with rage and he grabbed my face and kissed me hard and fast, his eyes searching mine to try and assure his inner beast that I really was okay. "You're fine? You smell like Dante, and others," he growled.

"Yeah, I'm fine. I promise."

"You were handcuffed to a bed?" he growled.

"Home, shoes," I reminded him. "I will tell you everything."

He pulled back and looked me up and down. "What the hell are you wearing?"

"I think it looks good," Dante said from behind me, earning a growl from Logan and an agreeing growl from the now five Werewolves flanking him.

"Go on," Logan told the Wolves, and they all slunk away, disappearing easily into the shadows. "Thank you for getting to her first, Dante," Logan said grudgingly.

"Luckily Anthea and I were already nearby searching with Drake and Zin when her father called to ask for our help getting here."

"You were searching for me already?"

"Of course. The entire city was on alert for your disappearance," Dante said.

That was embarrassing. The city's Supernatural P.I. had been missing, how the hell was anyone going to trust me with anything after this? "Is there a vehicle nearby? I need to get home and you need to not be arrested for indecent exposure," I pointed out to Logan. Inside the lobby the front desk attendant was on the phone gesturing wildly.

"Down this way," Dante said and hurried off.

We followed, Logan shifting back to wolf in a shadow so he would draw less attention and Anthea shifted as well. Now we just looked like a Prostitute walking with her pimp and his wolfdog.

Sirens in the distance were getting closer and we hurried along to where Dante's car was parked. Anthea was already in the driver seat, thankfully dressed. She was a fast flyer.

"I love your dress, Fawn, where did you get it?" Anthea asked as we all jumped in.

"Oh, well I hope I didn't steal it," I muttered.

Logan jumped in but stayed in wolf form, which I appreciated. I knew he was super comfortable with his nudity, but I wasn't, especially when in a car with his ex-fiancé.

I told them the whole story as we drove, and Logan growled when I got to the part about planning to help Rusty rather than just arrest her and throw her in my father's basement.

"She's guilty of something, but we can't let her fiancé rot as a rabbit and if Allen's really behind the worst of it, we can get him for it too. No one's getting away free and clear," I assured him and he harumphed in the cutest wolfy way. I bent down and kissed his snout. "I love you," I whispered as I rubbed my face against his furry cheek. The rumble of his chest was response enough to warm me.

When we got home, Betina, Jasmine, and Annabel ran out of the house greeting me and chastising me for running out of the store without them. After we hugged and I assured them I was fine, Annabel handed me a receipt for the dress.

"One-fifty for this! Everyone thought I was a prostitute. Which probably saved my life, but still," I grumbled.

"I like it," Logan whispered in my ear and ran a hand down over my ass.

"I think it's lovely," Dante agreed.

"Whorish," Evie said, not beating around the bush even a little. "You can't wear that outside of the bedroom, Fawn. Logan, you can't allow her out of the house like that."

I'd never heard her be so blatant.

"It's a party dress!" Anthea said with enthusiasm. "Just don't wear it to my wedding," she added with a harsh look.

"Well it's mine now, whether I like it or not, but I'll find something else to wear to the wedding. Something that shows more personality than skin," I said and flicked my gaze at Dante who smiled.

Anthea grinned at that, flashing her fangs as she followed us inside, apparently, they were staying. Not that I could argue after they'd just saved me.

"Annabel, I'm going to probably need your help with undoing some kind of curse," I said.

"Were you cursed?" She gasped and narrowed her eyes at me, no doubt feeling for a curse on my aura.

"Not me, a rabbit. You'll see when Rusty gets here with her fiancé." I explained the situation again and despite their grumbles about me being a softy, they couldn't argue with the fact that Peter didn't deserve to be a rabbit for the rest of his life, thief or not.

Fifteen minutes later I was throwing my new dress into the hamper and despite Logan's best efforts to keep me naked, I was dressed in jeans and a t-shirt, ready for Rusty to come by with her fiancé.

"She could be tricking you," Logan pointed out.

"She could have told Allen who I was," I reminded him. "She sought me out, she knew when I followed her into that garage that I was in charge of part of the city. She needed my help but was afraid to ask for it out in the open. It's not her fault Allen was there to interrupt us having a conversation. She panicked. I can't blame her for that."

Logan growled but didn't argue further. He stalked across the room and pulled me into his arms, playfully biting my neck. "If she tries anything, I'll eat them both."

"That's the plan," I said with a giggle. "Now let me go so I can get the cats outside; they might not react well to having a rabbit in the house."

Chester tweeted a confused tweet from his perch on the bed.

"You'll see, Chester, like a cat only different." He seemed curious.

Chapter Nineteen

When Rusty arrived with a familiar rabbit in her arms; one grey ear and a black circle around its left eye, it was just me, Logan, and Annabel. I didn't think she'd appreciate an audience, so I'd sent Dante and Anthea out into the night and Terrance had taken Jasmine and Betina for ice cream.

Logan eyed Rusty and the rabbit warily when they came in, but the look of fear and hope on Rusty's face was enough to convince him to at least hear her out.

"Rusty, this is Logan, my boyfriend," I said carefully, not feeling like the word quite fit but I really hated the word mate, and we weren't technically engaged either.

Logan grunted at the word but didn't correct me, just nodded at Rusty.

"And this is my friend Annabel. I'm hoping she can help reverse the curse on Peter. She's a very talented Witch."

"Thank you," Rusty gushed, eyes full of tears as she hugged the rabbit close. "Thank you for helping us."

Evie popped in with a smile, ready to greet whoever had shown up. "Oh, now we are letting rabbits in the house," she said then popped back out, apparently, she wasn't a rabbit fan.

"Can I see him?" I asked, reaching out for Peter. He looked like a regular rabbit, same as all the others hopping around the city, but he felt different. I could read him, unlike the zombie ones.

"He's very friendly," she assured me as she handed him over.

I held him up and looked into his eyes. I had a feeling I'd seen this rabbit before. Outside my garage actually. Had he been trying to get me to help him all this time? I wonder if he'd been the one on my porch that had attacked Logan. I glanced Logan's way and he was looking at the thing curiously, perhaps wondering the same thing. "So you can bring rabbits back from the dead, huh," I questioned, not expecting him to answer.

He made a little squeak *yes* and I smiled.

"Well hello, Peter. What happened to you?"

I listened as he squeaked, grunted, and squealed out his story in simple terms. Then sat back and handed him to Rusty. It was like when Logan or another Werewolf communicated with me, I could get the words they were trying to tell me rather than just the feeling behind it like I got from regular animals. Much more complete thoughts and sentences.

"What the hell did he say?" Logan asked.

"He said that Allen took his lucky rabbit's foot. Do you know what that means? He has all four feet." I checked again, just in case.

Rusty nodded eagerly. "Peter used to carry around a rabbit's foot keychain, but I'm not sure how that could be related to this."

"I think Allen used it in the spell. It's the key to keeping Peter from shifting back," I explained.

Peter squeaked agreement.

Annabel perked. "He could have transferred Peter's power into the object, especially if Peter was already connected to it."

"That's a nasty trick," I whispered.

"Yes, it is," Annabel agreed. Taking the power from another Magician was a death sentence offense. If that's what Allen had done, he was going to fight hard to keep us from catching him. He wasn't looking at a year in a cell for petty theft, and that made him very dangerous.

I met Logan's gaze briefly and he looked just as worried. We would have to be very careful.

"We'll need it I assume, to return his power to him."

Annabel nodded.

"Do you have any idea where it is now?" I asked Rusty.

"Something that important he'd probably keep close. I bet it's on him at all times," Rusty said. "He doesn't trust me, so he'd never leave it where I might find it by accident, or Peter." She looked at the rabbit in question. "Is that why you've refused to leave him?" she asked the rabbit.

He grunted affirmative and I interpreted for everyone.

"Great, so we need to strip search the guy," I said sarcastically.

"That could be fun!" Annabel said with a laugh.

I doubted it, but it also gave me an idea we could work with. I smiled brightly at Annabel. "Annabel, how do you feel about going undercover?"

"Like I said, this could be fun," she said with a grin.

I loved that she was always up for helping me, no matter how weird the request.

Logan grunted and crossed his arms over his chest already not liking where this was going.

"Before we plan anything though, what are Allen's powers? He can control the dead rabbits and he can portal through solid walls. Anything else? Oh and make you pass out, or go into a state of unconscious activity," I said with distaste.

"No, that's all he's got unless you count assholery as a superpower."

Sometimes I thought most Magicians had that one actually.

"Perfect, then I say we catch him with one of the oldest tricks in the book," I said with a grin.

We called in Anthea to help as well. The plan was simple enough. Allen liked to hang out at the hotel bar, and he was particularly attracted to slutty girls. Not a problem for Annabel or Anthea to pull off. They just had to pretend they were a couple supernaturals passing through town and flirt with the other obviously supernatural person in the bar. It wouldn't be that unusual and given the opportunity, one of them should be able to search the guy for the rabbit's foot. No one should have to actually get physical and both women were capable of protecting themselves against one Magician.

The hope was, we could get the foot and then arrest him. My fear was that if he got wind of our plan he might just run or refuse to cooperate. Once you were staring down a death sentence, you didn't always decide to give up more damming evidence of your crimes and a Magician turned Rabbit didn't make the best witness. If he didn't have the foot on him, we were arresting him anyway and hoping for the best.

Maybe he could bargain for a life sentence by reversing the spell on his brother willingly. I was hoping to not have to negotiate with another psychopath though. Hopefully, the girls could work their sexy magic.

"Yes! Be right there," Anthea squealed into the phone when I called. I think I heard Kearne in the background rumbling, likely in disapproval. It didn't seem like Anthea cared about his opinion though.

I hung up and looked at Logan. "I hope I'm not making an enemy of Kearne."

He shrugged. "Anthea is her own creature. If Kearne has agreed to marry her, he's accepted that."

I thought he was probably right.

I grabbed my stun gun and pepper spray and was ready to take down an asshole criminal.

Logan and I set up in a dark corner of the bar. I had my back to the rest of the room so Allen wouldn't see me, and Logan scanned the crowd with a scowl.

"You are going to scare everyone away," I teased. "If the bar is empty except for us and the girls, he's going to know something's up," I chastised for the third time.

"I don't like this plan," he said for the tenth.

"And what do you suggest we do instead, big man?" I teased, running my finger seductively around the rim on my wine glass. I batted my lashes at him and licked my lips.

It was no use; he wasn't paying me any attention. His scowl deepened. He didn't have a better idea; he'd tried to come up with one the whole drive here.

He'd had some reasonable demands that none of us argued with though. Neither of the girls was to go up to a room alone with the guy. Which shouldn't be too much of an issue, they were supposed to make it obvious they were looking for a threesome.

Who would turn that down?

"What if he decides to go upstairs first and check on you?"

"He won't. Rusty texted him and told him to meet her at the bar."

Rusty and Peter were in the hotel, but not in the bar, they were waiting in a room we'd rented for them to hide in, with Betina, Tony, and Dante there as bodyguards. No chance for them to just disappear while we were distracted. If somehow this was all a weird trick, they were not getting away from those three.

Overall, I felt pretty good about the plan I'd come up with. The piece I worried the most about was his little trick of making someone pass out. We needed to counteract it. Annabel made a quick charm for herself and Anthea. There was no way to test it and no guarantee it would work, but hopefully it would keep them from passing out because of whatever Allen was able to do. It was a hastily done spell, which left me with doubts.

"What if he doesn't show?" Logan asked again as he downed half his beer in one go.

There was the other big worry I had about this whole thing. Rusty telling him to meet her here didn't guarantee he would. What if he somehow sensed the trap and ran out of town while we sat and waited here like a bunch of idiots. "Then we regroup, I guess." I tried to sound confident, as if there'd be a sliver of a chance for us to find him if he really wanted to go disappear into the world for a while.

Logan grunted and scanned the room again.

Luckily, we didn't have to worry about that scenario. A couple minutes later, Allen waltzed in, and he noticed our girls right away. No surprise though, all the males in the room had noticed, and half had approached. Annabel was dressed in a tight black miniskirt and a leather bra under a purple mesh top. Anthea was wearing red leather leggings and a black bustier top. They looked like prostitutes to the humans I was sure, but anyone who knew Witches and Vamps would know this was a normal night out look for them.

Logan had already paid off the bartender and manager to not call the cops on the two. It wasn't exactly the type of look the hotel wanted to encourage, especially after the naked man out front incident earlier. I'd heard a few people talking about it, luckily, they weren't able to recognize Logan as the pervert. The manager and bartender probably thought Logan was the girls' pimp, but enough money exchanged hands to convince them to look the other way, at least for now.

The girls didn't acknowledge Allen right away and he didn't approach them immediately, though Logan said his eyes dipped over them both thoroughly a couple times. He was giving me the play by play.

"Annabel noticed him," Logan said behind his glass. "She's stretching now, really playing up her assets to lure him over."

"Of course she is," I said with a grin.

"Allen is ordering a drink near them, and Anthea turned to give him a quick eye."

"Is he falling for it?"

"Hasn't stopped looking at them," Logan confirmed. "He's got his drink now and he's approaching them."

It was killing me to not look. But I wouldn't risk them, or this plan. "What now?" I demanded.

"We have landing," Logan said with a laugh, enjoying his bout as a spy.

"Which one is he talking to?"

"He looks like he's interested in Annabel. Probably leery of Vamps."

"Smart," Witches were notoriously slutty and less likely to steal your blood than Vamps.

"He's buying them shots."

"That's a surefire way to a girl's crotch," I laughed, and Logan nearly choked on his beer.

"Is that right?"

I shrugged and gave him a wink as I sipped my wine.

"They're dragging him to the dance floor. Maybe they'll be able to pickpocket him there."

"I hope so." Could it be that easy?

It wasn't that easy.

Logan described their gyrating and groping with disgusting detail but in the end the three of them walked out of the room together.

"Damnit," I hissed and pulled out my phone to text Betina. *Three bees buzzing up the stairs.* Betina had insisted on the code words, despite the fact that it was a text with no chance of someone else overhearing. What was a stakeout without codewords though really?

"I don't like this," Logan said and called the waitress over. "Two shots of tequila."

I laughed as she walked away. "Logan, are you trying to get into my panties?" I asked with mock shock.

"Every goddamn day of my life," he said seriously.

We took the shots and waited anxiously. Thirty minutes later I texted Betina that we needed to hit plan C. *Fluff the pillow.*

Five minutes later, Betina knocked on their door pretending to be housekeeping, while we stood down the hallway just far enough away to be able to pretend we weren't watching.

"Housekeeping," Betina called in a high falsetto.

Nothing.

I met Betina's gaze down the hall and nodded. She knocked again.

Nothing.

"Damnit, Fawn I knew this was a mistake," Logan growled and stomped down the hallway.

"As if you had a better idea," I hissed and hurried to catch up. Dante and Tony came swooping in from the other end of the hallway with Rusty who used her keycard to let us all in.

"Fuck!" I grunted as I looked around the empty room.

"My daughter has been kidnapped days before her wedding," Dante said with an icy frown. Fear slid over me and I wanted to crumple even though he wasn't even looking at me.

I grabbed Logan's arm.

"We'll find her," Logan assured Dante, but I could see fear in Logan's eyes as his gaze swept the empty room. Not just because if we didn't, there'd be hell to pay, but because two women he cared about were in danger.

We didn't have a contingency plan for this.

"I know where they are," I said, meeting Rusty's eyes across the room. She was fearfully gripping her fiancé rabbit. She nodded.

Chapter Twenty

We raced through the city to the cemetery where he'd held me. Rusty directed because I'd been magically passed out both trips to and from the place. It was an old cemetery, maybe the oldest in all of Seattle, the Comet Lodge Cemetery. Luckily it was right in the middle of town, and we were there quickly. Finding the particular tomb would have been harder than I wanted to think about for Logan on scent alone. Logan said he didn't have any sense of smell through the thick cement. He could smell up to the area, but if he didn't know, he would never think there was a living being inside there. He'd have assumed something took them by flight straight up high enough to lose the scent.

Logan, Tony, and Dante got to work with the sledgehammers Logan had thankfully had in his work truck. Despite Dante's slender form he wielded it just as quick and fierce as Logan and Tony. Betina and I kept an eye on Rusty the whole time as well as a watch on the surroundings, hoping no neighbors would come to investigate or call the police reporting graverobbers.

It wasn't long before a small hole went all the way through the thick wall and Annabel's voice called out.

"That asshole is going to die a horrible slow burning death!"

"Annabel, you're okay! Is Anthea in there? Did you already kill Allen?"

"If he was in here, he'd be bleeding and officially a eunuch," Anthea snapped.

"Are you unharmed little bat?" Dante asked and the emotion in his voice made me shiver.

"I'm fine, Daddy, just pissed off," Anthea called back.

Unfortunately Allen hadn't fallen for our trap. I don't know when he'd seen through it, but he hadn't fallen for it, and I wasn't sure what to do from here.

"Shit," Rusty hissed, looking a little frantic. "He knows, he knows and he's going to kill me. He'll take Peter and kill me," she cried.

We all ignored her for the time being. Betina put an arm around me for comfort as the men continued their assault on the tomb wall. When the hole was large enough, Logan and Dante helped Annabel and Anthea out of the tomb. They both looked annoyed but otherwise unharmed.

"When did he figure it out?" I asked after they were over the rubble.

"I'm not sure. We got upstairs and then things went black," Annabel grumbled. Obviously upset that someone had gotten the upper hand on her and the charms she'd been confident in had failed.

I nodded, I'd experienced the same thing, twice.

"He was gone when we woke up here about five minutes before you guys started banging," Anthea added.

"Why didn't this work?" Annabel grumbled as she slipped the offending charm from around her neck. "It should have worked against any spell."

"Maybe because it isn't a spell, it's not magic like the Witches use, it's an innate ability he has," I shrugged. I hadn't wanted to mention it before because I didn't have a solution, but I'd worried about that exact thing.

"So what the hell do we do now?" Logan demanded.

All eyes turned to Rusty who was standing on the outskirts of the group looking worried.

"Where is he now, what is he going to do next?" I asked.

Rusty bit her lip. "I hope he isn't making a run for it. If he figured out that I'm working with you guys then he might have taken off without me. But he'll hunt me down eventually, he won't let this betrayal go." She looked down at the rabbit in her arms. "And I can't save Peter," she cried.

"Did anyone notice the absolute lack of rabbits when we rushed through town," Logan pointed out then.

"Fuck," I hissed. This was bad.

"We have to stop him. Peter can't be stuck like this forever," Rusty insisted.

"How the hell are we going to stop him, we don't even know which direction he might be headed," Dante pointed out. "We would need to stop all exits and I don't think we can organize that fast even if we *could* call in the manpower. Or wolfpower," he added, glancing at Logan.

An idea struck me, and I gasped. "Maybe we don't start with man or wolf power," I said excitedly. "Annabel, get Dexter to go to the Needle and call up a hell of a storm. We need all exits locked down. No one leaves the city."

Understanding lit up the faces around me. It may not be a great plan, but we had nothing else, and I wasn't about to just let this guy take his demon rabbits to plague another city.

Annabel was on the phone even as we hurried back to the truck. Logan and Dante too were making calls. We would need everyone out searching once we got the traffic stalled.

"How are we going to apprehend him if he can just put anyone he wants to sleep?" I grumbled.

"A spell to counteract his ability is useless," Annabel hissed as she hopped in the front seat of Logan's truck with me. She'd hung up with Misty, telling her to bring Dexter and a few other girls for support to the Space Needle.

"We need to snare his mind before he can even think to use his ability," Anthea said. "But Vamp powers of mind control require up close and personal work," she frowned.

Ensnaring a mind from a distance! I looked at Annabel, I think we both had the same thought at the same time. "Jason!"

"Damnit, I really don't want to see him right now," Annabel whined. "Maybe ever again."

"As if you have that choice. Tony get the boat ready and you two can get Jason while Misty and Dexter call in the storm. As soon as we have a lead on where Allen is, we get Jason there to ensnare his stupid little brain."

"Then what? Can Jason keep up the singing until he's locked in your father's basement?" Logan pointed out.

"Maybe, but just in case, we'll need some cuffs from my father like we used to catch Stephan. We get them on Allen, and he'll be helpless. Jason can go back home and out of your life," I assured Annabel.

"That's a lot of moving pieces," Dante pointed out.

"I know," I gritted and fired off a text to my father. And it meant we needed to separate, so we headed back to my place for everyone's cars. Annabel went with Tony, Betina happily tagging along. Logan and Dante both went to meet with their men and organize the searches. Everyone would have orders to find and track and report, not to engage so that no one ended up passed out and

Allen couldn't slip away. I needed to go to my parents' to get the cuffs.

Misty and her coven were taking Dexter to the Space Needle, and they would help him create the massive storm.

We had a plan and it felt as solid as we could get it. My phone dinged when I was almost to my parents' house. It was Rex.

You have the Supes working together on this... good.

I think that's as close to approval as I was going to get from my oldest brother. I'd take it. Of course if the plan failed, he was going to blame me entirely.

As I pulled up to the front of my parents' house the first flakes were starting to fall.

The storm was massive. Everything immediately shut down. People were stranded on roads and bridges; no boats or ferries could run. No one would be able to leave Seattle unless they tried on foot and that would be extremely dangerous. The temperatures plummeted to below freezing within fifteen minutes while ice and snow swirled around in high winds. The news was playing in my parents' living room and it was on emergency alert, reporting that it was the storm of the century, and no one should travel unless it was an emergency.

It was just what we needed. Phase one complete. I just hoped that Jason had made it to shore before things got too crazy out there on the water.

Logan reported that all pack members who were within city limits were searching already and all pack members outside of the city were called in to circle the storm, looking for a Magician trying to escape with a horde of rabbits. Vampires from around the world who'd come for the wedding had joined the hunt. Dante made sure they knew that Allen had dared to kidnap the bride so they would be especially motivated for revenge. The streets were more dangerous than ever for humans, but luckily most of them weren't venturing out into the storm. I didn't even want to be out in it, but I had no choice, this was my mission, and I was going to see it through. No one came into my city and set zombie rabbits out to steal from its citizens. They may have targeted humans, but that was almost worse. The risk of exposure of supernaturals for this was high and unacceptable.

So as much as I wanted to stay in the warm safety of my parents' house, I had to head out with the cuffs.

"Your car is never going to make it," Rex said as I stepped off the porch. I could barely see him standing a few feet away because of the thick snow falling. He had driven a new large jeep with huge tires and a ridiculous number of lights mounted on top.

"We don't all drive little dick energy vehicles, Rex," I snapped.

He just laughed. "Come on, I'll get you there safely. Dad would have my ass if I let anything happen to his precious baby girl."

I wanted to complain, but he was right. My car was not going to make it past the driveway in this. Which was the whole point, we needed it to be too dangerous for transportation.

I hopped in, shivering and turning up the heater. "Oh heated seats," I said happily. I'd quickly changed into warmer clothes in anticipation of the storm, but that didn't mean I was warm enough.

Rex didn't say anything until we were out of the driveway. "I hope this little plan works."

I glared at him. *Little plan...*

His face broke into a smirk, and he glanced at me. "Okay fine, it's a great plan. And I hope it works. If we send our rabbit problem to another Magician's territory, someone is going to question our ability to hold the city.

We don't need to be challenged in the middle of an inheritance." He meant in the middle of him inheriting the city from our father. It was a natural time in the past for others to step in and challenge the new Magician in charge. It wasn't very common anymore, but it could still happen.

I thought of Jasmine's father or Maddox and shivered. If they decided taking over would get them what they wanted from Jasmine, I had no doubt they'd use any excuse.

"I know." Nothing we dealt with was just about us. Something Rex would never let me forget apparently.

"And this weather thing?" he asked.

"Dealing," I grumbled.

"Dad said you have it all under control and I should just *support* you."

I grinned and looked out the passenger window so he couldn't see. I didn't want to risk him kicking me out of the jeep in the middle of this snowstorm. It had to kill him to support me.

"I am going to be busy with politics, I won't have time for all these little problems."

Little problems!

"I'm glad you're capable, I might need to give you a little bigger slice of the city as I take over for dad."

"Why not Damien?" He was the second oldest and already in charge of a large portion of the area south of Seattle city center.

"We've been discussing the possibility of him taking on Portland," Rex said.

"What?" That was extremely dangerous. Portland didn't have a Magician in charge and recently some Werewolves had gotten other Supes together to try and rally support to come out to humans. It hadn't gone well but the city was a sort of mess right now.

"Yeah, which means I'll need to give Chase a larger settlement too."

Chase, my youngest brother and my closest sibling. He wasn't interested in being in charge, but he'd do what he needed for the family. My other two brothers, Max and Luke were idiots. They probably needed another fifty years to mature before they would be capable of any kind of real responsibility. But Rex would likely keep them close to him and have them run errands for him. Keep an eye on them and make them feel important. Maybe Rex wasn't a terrible brother.

It left a lot of city for Chase and me though.

"I can handle it," I finally said.

"Yeah, along with your *pack* duties?" he sneered. "Dad told me how you stepped in with Jasmine. If you're claiming on Logan's pack's behalf, then you're in deep. Where's your loyalty going to lie, Fawn?"

"My loyalty is to what's right and good," I snapped back.

"We'll see," he said, the rest of the drive was silent.

I wanted to accuse him of being jealous. I had so much more than him, and even Jasmine preferred the company of the wolf pack to him. He never would have stood up for her in the face of her husband and father. He had a loyalty to the politics and Jasmine's father was part of that. I wanted to tell him how poorly that made him look. It didn't matter though, the reality was, I needed him to worry about the politics, it kept us all safe.

"Fuck, power is out," Rex grumbled as the city suddenly plunged into darkness.

"How long can he hold this," I wondered.

"Hopefully long enough," Rex said and parked in the middle of the snow covered road.

I jumped out and pushed through the mess to get to the gathered crowd around the Space Needle.

Chapter Twenty-One

I embraced Annabel when I got there, happy to see she'd made it back. "How's it going? Where's Jason?"

"Tony and Annabel have him. We figured it made more sense for him to be closer to the city edges where Allen is more likely to be found."

That made sense, and farther away from Annabel was preferable for her too, I was sure. "And things here are going well? The storm is massive!"

"It's great. This is actually kind of fun. We aren't allowed to make this kind of an impact usually," she said and a few of her coven mates circling the Needle nearby nodded agreement.

It was scary how powerful they were, especially when they worked together. They had formed a tight circle around the Needle with Dexter in the center. He held the staff, a tall wooden thing, twisted and really unassuming. I wouldn't have picked it out on sight as an item of importance at all. He was mumbling and the Witches were humming. I could feel waves of power vibrating the whole area.

"It's a good thing no humans are wandering around, this is some freaky shit," I said.

"Very," Rex agreed.

Annabel just shrugged, a huge smile on her face. "This is amazing. He heard from the last of his crew earlier too. So we're confident we have the reverse spell worked out. After this, we stop the original spell, and that staff is going to your father for safe keeping."

I was glad I wasn't going to have to argue that. Every one of these Witches was enjoying the power and the practice, but they still recognized the need to keep things safe and secret. Some powers shouldn't be out in the world.

But if I wasn't here, if this was Portland and no levelheaded Magician was in charge, would they keep it? Would they use it freely?

It was a good thing Damien wanted to take over that city, dangerous though it was going to be for him.

"Thank the Gods for that," I chattered between shivering teeth. I was ready for a regular cool wet fall. I never would have thought I'd get tired of a heat wave, but mixed with these bouts of freezing, I wanted normal.

"Is that him?" Rex asked, motioning toward Dexter. "He's just a kid."

"Kids make mistakes. Will you go easy on him?" I asked.

Rex met my gaze, and I could tell he wanted to immediately say no. Magicians didn't go easy on law breakers. His gaze darted over to Dexter again and back to me. "We'll see what kind of real damage was done. At least he is going to fix it and he's helping with this."

I was satisfied with that for now and smiled at my brother. Maybe he wasn't going to be a terror in charge.

"Where's Rusty?"

"She's huddled in the car with Peter. Apparently, Peter isn't a snow rabbit," she laughed.

I pulled out my phone and stared at the blank screen. I really wanted an update, I wanted to know where to take the cuffs. I wanted to stop this terrible storm shutting down the city.

"Oh no, you can't get any service right here," Annabel said. "You need to go back like to the middle of the street to get anything."

I slogged back through the snow and stopped on the other side of the jeep, letting it block some of the wind as I pulled my phone out again. This time the screen lit up with life and I sent a message out to Logan and Dante asking for an update and letting them know I was at the Needle with the cuffs.

"You!" a voice snarled as it carried across the wind.

I turned just in time to see a hand reach out. I fell to the ground in defense, rolling through the snow and popping back up. The wind and jeep would cover anything going on from the others I realized as I stared at the glaring face of Allen. I grabbed my stun gun knowing that the pepper spray would never get to its intended mark with this wind, and I'd never get cuffs on him if he was fighting back. I didn't want to get close enough for him to make me blackout again though, so I waited, crouched and ready to run rather than fight.

My gaze darted around, no one was anywhere near, no one was going to notice until it was too late.

Allen took a sliding step forward. "I should have known you were involved. Rusty was far too concerned with me not killing you," he sneered. "Who the hell are you?

"I am Fawn Malero, Supernatural P.I. and the Magician in charge of half this city," I said proudly. "Give it up, Allen. You'll never make it out of my city."

"Why do you think I'm here? I plan to get a little insurance for my escape."

"Not going to happen. Your only chance is if you come quietly. My father is a fair Magician and so far, you haven't killed anyone, and you haven't let our secret out. You're looking at a jail sentence, not death." That would be true if it wasn't for the fact that he'd trapped his brother in rabbit form, but I wasn't going to mention that.

"Fawn Malero," he sneered. "I heard you were trying to make yourself a name here. Others are talking about the weak Magician taking charge of Seattle, can't even do it alone. Has to sleep with Werewolves and keep Trolls in order to survive," he scoffed.

"Fuck you," I snarled, taking the bait. I lashed out with my stun gun, but he sidestepped me no problem. "This is my city and I've got powerful friends behind me. You've just got dead rabbits. It doesn't make me weak to have people backing me up."

"But the dead listen so well," he said and within moments I was surrounded by rabbits.

I couldn't keep my balance as they scrabbled against my feet and legs. I pinwheeled my arms and fell back, thankfully the snow kept me from slamming my head against the pavement.

Allen jumped on me, his lips already moving, no doubt about to black me out again. Where the hell was Jason when I needed him? But I had been ready, I knew what was coming and as he landed on me, he was shot full of volts. He shivered and shook, then fell limp on me as blackness started to edge around my brain and eyes.

"Fawn!" Rex yelled, falling to his knees beside me and swiping at rabbits that surrounded us.

"Get him off me." I was soaked, pretty sure I'd been bitten, and on the edge of passing out from the power he'd started to hit me with.

Rex lifted the weight of Allen off me. I scrambled to get up, kicking at the rabbits still surrounding us and shaking my head to dispel the remaining lag.

"Are you okay?" Rex asked.

"I think so, tell Dexter to stop. It will signal that we've got him, and everyone can stop looking."

Rex ran off to do what I asked, and I turned with a satisfied smirk, cuffs in my hand. I slid them onto Allen's wrists as he started to grumble awake.

"You're done, fucker," I snarled in his ear.

"Am I?" He asked as I rolled him to his back. His eyes opened and he looked at me with something that made my skin prickle. "Where's Rusty?" he asked.

I frowned at him, not understanding at first. She'd been huddled in a car with Pete, waiting it out.

"You didn't think I wouldn't have one last trick up my sleeve, did you?"

"What did you do?"

He laughed and I kicked his side as hard as I could, satisfied by his grunt of pain.

"You're digging your hole deeper, asshole."

"I put her and my idiot brother away, if you want to save her, you'll have to let me go."

I looked around, desperate to see Rusty safe somewhere. Then I saw the hotel with the parking garage where Anthea had lost the rabbits.

"You shoved her in the sewer, didn't you?" It probably wouldn't kill her, but it wouldn't be pleasant.

"Even better than that, no, there is a space behind a wall in that parking garage that I discovered is just big enough for a small woman and her rabbit fiancé. Not a lot of air though," he laughed. "You'll have to undo these, or I can't use my magic to save her."

Annabel ran over as the snow stopped and the wind settled. In the distance I heard the Werewolves howl as they alerted to the change, spreading the word that it was over.

But it wasn't.

"Rusty," I told Annabel as she skidded to a stop in the slush.

"What about Rusty? She's in the car?" Annabel asked.

"He put her in the wall," I whispered.

He stared up at us with such satisfaction on his face. The look of a true psychopath.

"Shit," Annabel hissed and kicked his hip.

"Her time is running out, ladies. It's her or me, you can't have us both."

Annabel looked at me and I froze. I couldn't sacrifice Rusty's life, but if I undid his cuffs he'd get away.

"What if he's lying," Annabel warned as I knelt beside him.

"What if he's not," I said without looking up at her. "How close is Jason?" Maybe we could use the siren power to make him do what we needed.

"I don't know," Annabel whispered and pulled out her phone, firing off a text.

"I knew you were too weak to do what needed to be done. She's a criminal too, but you're going to let me go to save her life. You don't deserve this city. Your father is weak for letting you play at being in charge and that's why people like me will keep coming in." Allen laughed and I gripped his cuffs, hating that he might be right.

"Not sacrificing lives isn't a weakness, it's what separates us from the beasts," I whispered as I undid the cuffs.

He jumped up and ran across the street. We followed.

"What the hell are you doing?" Rex called, chasing after us.

Allen ducked into the garage and went to a wall, disappearing within and back out seconds later with a limp Rusty, Peter clutched to her chest. I rushed to her and immediately felt for her injuries, her life force and anything else my healing powers might be able to fix. She was half dead, oxygen starved, and the last flicker of her mind was almost out. It reminded me of Betina after the lightning strike and tears stung my eyes as I poured everything I had into that little flame, willing it back to life. It sparked, it stuttered, and it fought to die, but I wouldn't let it. I held on, knowing that if I let her die and Allen got away, he'd be right, I couldn't make the right decisions for the city, and I shouldn't be in charge.

I pushed harder, I demanded her spark to light her body. I wasn't going to take no for an answer. It grew slowly, spreading like molasses through her mind and body, but it did it. By the time I pulled back, sweat was dripping down my face and I was shaking, but she was going to make it. I slipped my hands to the rabbit. There was a tiny spark in him, and it answered my magic eagerly, he wasn't ready to give up on life and it made me wonder why Rusty's had been so defiant. Was she so sure that her life was worthless, that she'd failed and would never have her love back? She had been willing to accept death. Peter was going to be okay, though I couldn't make him not be a rabbit, at least for now, he was going to live.

"You're both alright," I whispered to Rusty, hoping some part of her would hear me and start fighting harder to survive. "And we will get Allen, I swear that bastard is going to pay for all of this."

They needed a safe warm place to recover and be watched.

I whipped my head around, searching for help. Annabel was passed out and Rex was nowhere to be seen. Perhaps he'd taken off after Allen. I rushed to Annabel and laid my hands to her shoulders. She was fine, under Allen's sleep spell. I pushed my magic into her and forced her to wake up, amazed that I'd been able to do that.

Her eyes burst open, and she gasped. We stared at each other for a split second, then she jumped to her feet. "Asshole!" she screamed and we ran up and out of the parking garage. I pulled out my cell and called Terrance for help. He was with Jasmine at home, but they could get here fast and take care of Rusty and Peter, get them to my parents' house.

"We need everyone searching again," I said as I sent off a text to Dante and Logan. "He's not leaving this city. Get the storm back up, shut shit down."

Annabel hurried to deliver that message to Dexter and the coven while I waited with Rusty, I didn't have any great tracking abilities and if I couldn't trust the experts, I wasn't making the best decisions.

Chapter Twenty-Two

Terrance came squealing into the parking garage and loaded Rusty and Peter into his truck. Jasmine was in there bundled up and smiling. "Take them to my father, he's expecting you," I ordered. "Don't let her out of your sight. She's technically a prisoner."

"Are you okay?" Terrance asked. "Logan would kill me if I left you and you're injured."

"I'm fine," I assured him. "I need to see this guy caught. Hopefully, I'll be bringing him in to my father before the night's over. Wait there with Jasmine until the snow stops, these roads are dangerous."

"Yes ma'am," he mocked, then his face smoothed into a serious frown. "I believe you will succeed, Fawn, you're good at what you do." He hopped back into the truck. They drove out and I headed back up to the street. Annabel was standing with the coven and Dexter by the Space Needle and magic prickled on the air along with snowflakes and a harsh wind. Howls lit up the night spreading the message that things actually weren't over. The Vamps were out there as well, Allen wouldn't get away, everyone was circling closer, squeezing the Magician back here.

I had brought together the entire city of supernaturals, and some from out of town, I was *not* too weak for this, I was exactly what the city needed.

Unless this didn't work. But I couldn't think about that now.

After about thirty minutes, in which time I vacillated between full belief that I was right and certainty that I was wrong about a hundred times, my phone rang with good news. They had him cornered in a park. There were too many for him to get away by making one or two pass out. But they couldn't safely detain him, so they were waiting.

I needed to get there, preferably with Jason to sing him to submission and I would cuff the bastard. I didn't trust he'd fall on my stun gun again.

"Shut it down!" I called to Annabel who relayed the message. Her coven and Dexter's tone changed, their message out to direct the magic became something smoother. Working to reverse the original spell, I assumed.

Annabel and I took Rex's jeep and headed toward the park. "Get Jason there," I said as we slid around corners and nearly took out more than one car that had been abandoned during the storm.

"He's going to want to talk about our relationship again," she grumbled.

"So tell him you can be friends. He's useful apparently, so maybe don't hurt his feelings too badly in the process."

"Easy for you to say, he isn't in love with you," Annabel said, but she sent directions to Tony and Betina.

By the time we pulled up to the park, the weather was clear and cool, it felt amazingly normal. Allan had managed to knock out a couple Werewolves and Vamps when they'd first cornered him, but after that, everyone stayed back, and he remained in the middle of their circle shouting threats like a madman. Rabbits swirled around inside and outside of the circle, much to the annoyance of everyone. But they couldn't really do much to help Allen.

My gaze found Logan first, like a magnet, my eyes sought him out in any crowd. Rex was there too, he must have chased Allen on foot. Without him chasing, who knows if Allen would have been able to evade everyone. With his ability to go through walls it was a wonder they'd managed to trap him, but it wasn't surprising that it had ended up being in such an open space. Nowhere for him to slip into.

"Now what?" Logan asked after he pulled me in for a hug and deep kiss.

"I think we need to wait for Jason, he's close." I held up the cuffs. "Then it's all over."

"Easy," Logan said with a grunt.

It hadn't been easy so far, but hopefully this part would be.

"This has been an interesting visit to your city," Cassius said, practically floating as he approached us.

"I'm sorry it wasn't more pleasant," I said, managing to keep my voice steady. It helped that I was close to Logan, he gave me strength. "I am glad it will be all cleared up before your granddaughter's wedding though."

"Indeed," he said and left.

"I'm not sure if he's actually happy or not," I whispered to Logan.

"I have a feeling he's not sure either," Logan whispered back.

I went to work on the couple of passed out Supes, waking them up easily to the impressed gazes of those watching. Even Rex nodded approvingly.

When Tony and Betina arrived with Jason, everyone was sick of hearing the baseless threats Allen was spewing. It was like watching a toddler throw a tantrum. There was no reasoning with him, you just hoped he'd tire himself out soon and take a nap.

Jason didn't hesitate to start singing. His song filled the night air and prickled me but it was directed at Allen, so I felt no extra draw to the man. I did notice Annabel shift uncomfortably and wondered if it was reminding her of their passionate time together.

The circle surrounding Allen parted as the Magician fell silent, staring at Jason. I followed Jason to Allen who sat when we got close, a glazed look of adoration on his face. I smiled and threw the cuffs on him with a whispered *Fuck you*.

"Shut it down, Jason," I said. I wanted Allen to know how he'd been bested.

As soon as Jason stopped singing, Allen woke up and he was pissed. But he was helpless, and I grinned as Logan hauled him up by his arm and dragged him to Rex's jeep.

There were a few cheers as we went and I felt like a bit of a celebrity. I could get used to this.

Jason was surprisingly silent the whole drive to my parents' house and I started to worry he wasn't going to tell us where the rabbit's foot was. I would really hate to tell Rusty it had all been a bust, and poor Peter would remain a rabbit until someone figured out how to break the spell.

Once in a cell with my father glaring at him with authority and explaining what he would be charged with, and threatening him with an uncomfortable strip search, Jason was convinced to give up the rabbit's foot.

"This will do it," he said, pulling on a chain around his neck. A white rabbit's foot hung from it like a lucky charm.

"That's just weird," Stephan commented from his cot a few cells over.

"All I have to do is put it near him?" I asked, not trusting this willingness to be helpful.

"Yes, he just needs to touch it and the powers will transfer back to him. The foot itself isn't magic, I was just able to use it to hold his magic because he valued it," Allen explained and handed it through the bars.

I took it and glanced at my father who gave a slight nod, apparently it sounded reasonable to him though I'd never heard of such a thing.

Stephan whistled. "That's a powerful kind of magic."

"Shut up," I hissed at Stephan. Then glared at Allen. "Don't get too comfortable with your roomy over there, he's on death row. He'd slit your throat if it gave him a chance at freedom."

"Imminent death makes a man desperate," Allen said quietly and glanced over and across at Stephan who was now standing at the bars of his own cell.

"Why were you in Seattle?" I asked, hoping it wasn't because we seemed weak and easy to invade.

"Why would I tell you, I'm going to die for my crimes," Allen scoffed. "Death row prisoner number two."

"True, and you have nothing of value to trade for a stay of execution. It is only curiosity that has me still here asking." And the need for a little reassurance.

Allen gripped the bars; his face was set in a wide grin and his eyes were half lidded as he glared at me. "I came because I know you're weak. You saved Rusty and my idiot brother, letting me escape. It proves your weakness is your empathy for those weaker than you. Everyone saw it and you had to call in Vamps and Weres to help you, couldn't catch me on your own. You won't always have so many others to call on for help."

He was right, if it hadn't been for the wedding party in town, he might have gotten away, the extra eyes had been a huge benefit tonight, but I wasn't going to let him know how his words filled me with fear. "I have friends in powerful places, Allen. You are the puppet master of rabbits." I turned and walked away, not missing the smile of approval on my father's face.

"Do you think he's telling the truth?" My father asked when we got upstairs and the door was closed behind me.

"I am afraid he is." If I was tested alone, I wouldn't stand a chance.

Betina, Tony, Logan, Annabel, Terrance, and Jasmine were standing in the hall watching us. I wasn't alone, I reminded myself.

"We'll be ready for any challenges that may come," my father said firmly. "You did the right thing, all around, Fawn. I have no doubt that you're right for this position and Rex is coming round to the idea too. Everyone saw how well you set things in motion. Brains behind the operation is just as important as the brawn pulling it off. Two arms of the same beast."

I glowed under his praise, and it lifted some of my doubts, but not all. I wasn't sure anything could.

I held up the foot. "Let's meet Peter."

Rusty was recovering in a guest bedroom guarded by Damien and Luke. My mother hovered, wanting to make sure Rusty was comfortable, if she wasn't in a jail cell, she was a guest not a prisoner, my mother said.

Rusty not being in a jail cell was just a technicality, but I knew better than to argue with my mother about proper hostess etiquette.

Rusty was sleeping still, but Peter looked at me with his beady rabbit eyes.

"Hey, I think this belongs to you," I said and held up the foot. He hopped off the bed and to my feet eagerly. I set the foot next to him and watched in fascination as he touched it with his nose and transformed into a man. Naked and looking almost exactly like his brother. Which made sense, they were twins. But Peter was a little bulkier, with a little scruffier hair, and a partial beard.

He stretched and clapped and laughed. "Oh fuck, this feels good," he said quietly, trying not to wake Rusty.

He pulled me in for a hug which had Logan growling a warning behind me, then Peter hurried to kneel beside Rusty.

"Wake up love, I'm back," he said and gently stroked the hair away from her face.

Rusty didn't open her eyes. Peter looked at me, worried.

"She's okay, but she needs time to recover. She was pretty far gone after we pulled you guys out of the wall."

"That bastard doesn't care who gets hurt," Peter hissed. "Never has. I was always pulling him back from the edge of too far."

"Which is why he made sure you couldn't anymore," I said.

"He's my brother, but he is nothing like me. When I told him I was going to marry Rusty he freaked out. He thought I was going to leave him; I suppose I would have eventually."

I didn't know what to say to that.

My father brought in some clothes then, so I didn't have to respond. Peter dressed quickly, then we took him to my father's office for a talk so Rusty could continue resting in quiet.

"Am I under arrest?" Peter asked stiffly.

My father took a heavy breath. "Technically we don't have proof that you committed any crimes," my father said.

His words shocked me, and I stared at him as he continued.

"From what I've seen, you were forced to act in a certain manner because your magic was taken. Your fiancé had no choice but to go along because your life was threatened. You both sought out my daughter's help, did you not?"

"I-I did, we did," he stuttered out and looked at me with wide eyes.

"Okay, well then I expect all items that have been stolen will be returned once Rusty is recovered," my father said sternly, one eyebrow lifted as he looked at Peter.

"Yes, of course, Sir," Peter said quickly.

Rex was going to be pissed about my father's decision.

"I will expect you two to stick around until after Allen's trial. I will expect you both to stand witness as to his actions and I expect all zombie rabbits out of my city, tonight."

Peter nodded frantically and snapped his fingers. "Done, they are released."

"And their bodies?" I questioned skeptical of his wording.

"Yeah, sorry they just drop where they are at. The human city will have to clean them up, but luckily, I think the weather will be blamed for their deaths, it won't be suspicious," Peter said.

My father didn't look overly pleased but nodded. "You can't tell them to leave the city because Allen has that part of the power?" he asked.

"Yeah, it's really kind of a crappy power all on its own," Peter admitted.

"Then I think we've done the best we can here," my father said, and it was an obvious dismissal. I held the door open and Peter hurried out of the office and back to the room Rusty was resting in.

"You will make sure they hold up their end of the bargain," my father said when the door to Rusty's room shut. "All items must be returned anonymously."

"I understand." I looked at my dad and frowned. "Why are you being so..." I didn't want to say fair, but that's what it felt like. "Lenient?" I settled on.

He sighed. "I was reminded recently of how I want my city to run, and it isn't in the image of the old ways. I think part of that is letting people make up for some of their mistakes. Dexter is another case that I'm considering. In reality if I were to hold him accountable, I would need to hold every one of his friends accountable too. But kids playing with something that they thought was fake, then getting scared." He shrugged. "I think they've all learned their lessons and the damage has been fixed."

"Wow." I didn't know what else to say. "I think that makes a lot of sense, Dad."

"I want to show Rex a different way to handle the city."

I had a feeling he also wanted to show Portland that a city ruled by a Magician wasn't necessarily a scary ordeal. Smoothing the way for Damien to take over and put in some reasonable rules. My father was a smart man, and for the first time, I realized how very fair and thoughtful.

Chapter Twenty-Three

The day before Anthea's wedding, Maddox made a show of standing in front of my house looking like a total creep. I had gotten Annabel to reinstate the wards covering me, Betina and Jasmine so he couldn't cross onto the property unless he made another earthquake and I had warned him that if he did that, it would be taken as a threat against the lives of everyone in my house.

He didn't want the consequences of that.

It had still taken Logan and Tony both to keep Terrance from walking out there and ripping the idiot apart as Jasmine cried. I think mostly it was because of the pregnancy hormones, she wasn't thinking clearly or else she would have realized Maddox's whole plan was to upset her and set off Terrance into reacting so he could fight without being blamed for starting anything.

"We're leaving," Terrance declared when he was calmed down by Logan's alpha energy. I had never seen Terrance so ruled by emotions and it wasn't even close to the full moon. Which made me think he really was in love with Jasmine, and it wasn't just some weird pregnancy fetish attracting him to her. I was thankful for that proof.

"Leaving?" Jasmine asked, wiping tears from her eyes.

"Leaving," Terrance echoed. "We'll go to my place for a while and let Maddox stew in not knowing where you are. He doesn't deserve to be a part of your life." Terrance crossed the room and pulled her into his arms. "Let me immerse you in mine," he whispered against her neck.

I sighed, Evie sighed, Betina groaned, "Get a room."

"That's the plan," Terrance said and pulled away from Jasmine. "Now go pack," he said, slapping her ass when she turned.

"At least I'll get my room back," Betina said, but there was a sadness in her tone, she'd come to really like Jasmine and their late-night movie marathons.

I looked at Logan for assurance that this was a good idea. He put an arm around my back and kissed the top of my head. "Terrance will take care of her," he assured me.

"He better," I said, knowing Terrance could hear me. "But can he also take care of the baby when it comes?"

We didn't have an answer for that. There was going to be trouble when it was born.

"I guess I don't need this," Jasmine said as she came out of the room with a bag in one hand and the dress she'd bought for the wedding in the other. "I suppose I should let Rex know I can't go tomorrow."

"He'll get over it," I assured her. It wasn't as if they were dating. "Maybe we can find him someone else to attend with. Does Lila want to go?" I asked Logan.

Logan grunted. "I don't want my sister on a date with Rex, even if it is just as friends, she makes terrible choices, she'll probably fall in love."

I had to laugh because that was very true.

"I bet Kalina would go, she's back in town," Tony said.

I shrugged, seemed like a good choice. Tony's sister was a half Elf, half Witch. She was tiny and adorable and very sweet. I was certain my brother would enjoy her company and think that she would look good on his arm, which I believe is the biggest worry for him at the moment. Making an impression in the city he was going to rule.

I hugged Jasmine tight and promised I wouldn't stop thinking of ways to hide the child once it arrived. Then I gave Terrance another stern warning and watched them walk out full of smiles.

They were starting a life together I realized, and it felt permanent despite the uncertainty that surrounded the pregnancy and Maddox.

Rex was annoyed about the change when I told him, but he didn't let it show when he arrived to pick up Kalina. They hadn't met previously, and I saw a spark in his eyes when he gazed at her. She was beautiful in a floor length sage green gown that was cut low. She had her long white hair swept up in a fancy bun showing off her pointy ears and since she'd been visiting with her father's clan and getting Earth treatments, she looked vibrant and healthy.

Annabel was attending the wedding as a representative of her coven, Misty had no interest in such boring social affairs, or so she said. Annabel said she was not going to take any man who would get ideas, so Betina was her date. Both women were dressed immaculately in black. Annabel's dress was short with deep purple flowers embroidered on it and a mesh underlay that peeked out at the top and bottom. Betina wore a floor length black dress with a slit up to her thigh and a conservative neckline. It dipped low in the back showing off a striking amount of skin.. She looked like a goddess that could crush you if she chose. I think that was what she was going for. Working out with Logan was really starting to show in her musculature.

I, of course, attended with Logan, head held high and looking amazing in a floor length red dress that hugged my curves. A leaf pattern was embroidered in black around the bottom and vines snaked up to my waist. I wore Logan's mom's choker and knew I was making a statement. By the look of annoyance in Dante's eyes, I knew he was reading it clearly.

If I was going to embrace this city and the help of other supernaturals in it, I was also going to embrace my part of the pack that ruled so much of it and protected it's outer edges. My father had done a lot by himself, but that wasn't the way it had to be and while I was shaking things up in the supernatural world of Seattle, I was going to embrace the parts I loved the most. I loved Logan, a lot.

"Gorgeous as always," Dante said, kissing my cheek a little too long. "I do hope you save a dance for me."

What could I say but, "Yes, thank you, Dante."

Logan was a little stiff beside me, but he didn't argue. We weren't that kind of couple. There was plenty of trust between us.

We couldn't function any other way.

Drake and Zin were there of course. Drake looking handsome in an all-black tux and Zin turning heads in an ice blue flirty length dress that sparkled every time she turned and showed more than a little cleavage. Drake was going to have to keep her close or every single Vamp in the room was going to try and hit on her. I think he knew it too by the way he gripped her arm, and his face was in a slight scowl.

"You look amazing," I told Zin as I hugged her. "You're going to give poor old Drake a heart attack trying to keep the others away," I whispered in her ear.

She just giggled.

Music started to play, and we were all ushered into the main room. Drake and Zin moved to sit up front since they were family, but we were shown seats near the back, which didn't bother me. We weren't family and we weren't Vampires.

"This is extravagant," Kalina said quietly.

"Everything Vampires do is extravagant," Rex said.

Anthea walked in then and the whole room fell into silence. Her wedding dress was blood red and as wide as the aisle. She practically floated as she moved down it. I don't know why the princess style surprised me so much, after all she was Vampire royalty, but I didn't see her as such a girly type. Kearne was looking dapper in a traditional black suit and red tie. When they stood together under a canopy of black roses, I felt a little teary. They looked like a perfect match. I hoped they had a long and happy life together.

The ceremony was long and formal, ending in each Vampire biting into the other's ring finger instead of a kiss. They pulled the other's finger into their mouth, obviously drawing in blood in an overly dramatic show of swallowing. Then the fingers popped out of their mouths, and they finally kissed deeply, further mixing their blood I was guessing.

"Gag," Betina whispered beside me, and I had to agree, that was a little weird.

Logan leaned over to whisper in my ear. "Werewolves don't exchange blood like that in a wedding ceremony, but biting is encouraged," he teased.

Shit, I hoped he was teasing. "I suppose when Lila gets married I'll know if you're teasing," I said.

He grinned and grunted, knowing I was avoiding the obvious turn of that conversation. Marriage felt like something in the far future for us. In the future, yes, but far into it.

After the very formal affair of the ceremony, the reception was surprisingly light. It was really just a big party with loud music, dancing, food, and drink. Anthea removed the large skirt of her dress leaving her in a form fitting floor length dress with a slit up to the top of her thigh. I was surprised we couldn't see something inappropriate. It was equally as gorgeous as the full skirt version, but much more practical for moving among a crowd and much more her personality.

After a few songs Dante cut in and took me from Logan's grasp. I was swept into the crowd and lost sight of him immediately, which I didn't like.

"You are a wonderful tease, Fawn," Dante said, his eyes on my necklace.

"I am no such thing. I have never told you anything but the truth. I am in a committed relationship with Logan, and not a big fan of Vampires."

He laughed loudly and drew the attention of those around us.

"I dream of you in my arms," he said, his eyes intense as they bored into mine.

I swallowed, not willing to lie to him. I had a feeling he already knew what kind of dreams I had.

"Someday," he whispered in my ear when the song was over and then he delivered me back to Logan who was stepping off of the dancefloor with Betina.

"Is it too early to leave?" I asked Logan when I was once again settled against him.

"I think we've done our duty," he said.

We gathered our party and left. The night was crisp and damp, very normal for Halloween in Seattle. No rabbits hopped across our path as we walked to Annabel's car, something I never thought I'd have reason to be grateful for.

For the moment, my city was safe. I leaned into Logan's side and smiled up at his face. "What do you think about taking a little vacation to your cabin? A few days out of the city and all alone?" I asked, trailing a finger down his chest. Maybe I was jealous that Terrance and Jasmine were getting a little alone time in the woods, it sounded like heaven right now. And since Rusty and Peter had officially returned the last item taken yesterday and were only still in town waiting for Allen's trial, I was off duty until I decided to visit Stephan for my next mission, or another one fell onto my doorstep.

Another reason to get out of town, if I wasn't home, no one could knock on my door with trouble.

He rumbled under my touch, making me smile brightly. I loved the way I affected this man and hoped it would never wear off.

"I think that's the best idea you've ever had, Fawn Malero."

"Wait until you hear my next one. Jasmine told me a little more about what she witnessed Max doing in that hotel room. And Patty texted me just the other day to tell me her marriage has never been better."

Logan growled and pulled me tighter against him. "Fawn, I hope you're joking because I am far too alpha for what Max is into."

I laughed because I knew that was true and I loved him for it.

About the Author

Courtney Davis is a mother, wife and teacher who has always loved to find time to escape into a good story. She's been in love with reading and writing since she was a child and dreams of a life where she can devote herself fully to creating worlds and exploring relationships. To give someone else enjoyment through her words is the ultimate thrill.

Acknowledgments

I am forever grateful for the team at DXVaros publishing for helping to make my dream of writing a reality. Your continued willingness to work with me and publish Fawn's supernatural adventures is invaluable.

Thank you!

OTHER EXQUISITE FICTION FROM
DX VAROS PUBLISHING

Christopher Tuthill
THE OSPREY MAN

Larry F. Sommers
PRICE OF PASSAGE

Fidelis O. MkParu
SOULFUL RETURN

J.M. Stephen
THE EMERGENCE OF EXPANDING LIGHT

G.P. Gottlieb
CHARRED: A WHIPPED AND SIPPED MYSTERY

Eileen Joyce Donovan
THE CAMPBELL SISTERS

Karuna Das
SEX, DRUGS, AND SPIRITUAL ENLIGHTENMENT
(BUT MOSTLY THE FIRST TWO)

Felicia Watson
WHERE NO ONE WILL SEE

Jessica Stilling
AFTER THE BARRICADES

and many more available at
www.DXVaros.com or your favorite book seller

Milton Keynes UK
Ingram Content Group UK Ltd.
UKHW040636041023
429927UK00001B/30

9 781955 065894